"A thoroughly enjoyable read. *The Devil I Know* has it all with an unforgettable and intelligent heroine in Julia and real life, relatable characters. The story engages you from the start but continues to surprise and keeps you reading late into the night."

–KIM C.

"*The Devil I Know* is definitely not your average love story. It's an exhilarating tale of that forbidden love you have deep down for the always good-looking bad boy in life. I think every woman can relate to Julia in some way, and most men will want to relate to Adrian. The story never has a dull moment, has a ton of spunk and sass, and left me having a hard time putting the book down! You won't regret reading this new tale from Bess, and I already can't wait to see what she has in store for her next literary adventure."

–JENNIFER G.

"So, so good! I didn't want it to end! I loved that I couldn't ever predict what was going to happen."

–GERI M.

"I'm telling everyone it's even better than *Never the Same*, but right now I'm sitting here thinking about how sad I am to not have any more to read."

–RENEE R.

"The first chapter captivated me. I couldn't wait to see how the story ended and was sad when it did...I want more!! The thrill of the unknown and being in a world that you would never be involved in is exciting. I guess we all have a little of Julia in us. It's funny what you will do for love and where it will lead you. If you love to escape in a good book and are looking for the unpredictable and unexpected then you must read *The Devil I Know*. Bess Richards will not disappoint–I cannot wait for her next book!"

–LENA M.

"This is one of those books that you'll love so much you'll immediately want to flip back to the beginning and start all over again. And, the characters are so real, you'll actually miss them enough to do it."

–KARI R.

"This is the second book by Bess Richards that I've read. Enjoyed both! In *The Devil I Know*, it was easy to get pulled into the story of the characters' lives. The bad part of caring so much about a character in a story is the concern over what the next chapter will bring. Each chapter seemed to bring more questions and doubt about whether there would be a happy ending...or not. Give me a book any day that has some twists and turns and throw in some angst over what will happen to a character! This book fulfilled that."

–ANITA P.

"You will have a hard time putting this book down as you get involved with all of the changes in Julia's life that test her love and loyalty to self. All the twists and turns make this book very interesting to read."

–REBECCA G.

THE
DEVIL
I
KNOW

THE DEVIL I KNOW

A NOVEL

Bess Richards
bessrichards.com

Copyright © 2016 by Bess Richards

Published by House of Kiku

houseofkiku.com

Printed in the United States of America

2016 Paperback Edition

ISBN: 978-0-9967018-1-5

Author Photograph by Aislinn Kate Photography

Cover Design by Christian Fuenfhausen

Version_1

To the real Tony Two Guns—my Patrick, Mr. Shirley,
and Adrian all in one

Contents

PART ONE

ONE

Julia

WHY IS IT THAT we remember monumental days by their ordinary details? I've yet to make an official conclusion, but I recall a sticky booth and the formica table still damp with washcloth streaks. I could be describing a hundred regular days, but this day, even though I was in a very usual place, was out of the ordinary in an unfortunate way, and no pesky detail could make it worse, or even better.

I stared across our favorite table, the bench opposite me so solemnly empty as I meditated on the implications of what had happened just days before, the reason I was suffocating inside a sleek, black dress. The panty hose I'd bought at the very last minute were cutting into my waist, and as I wriggled left and right, using my still-shaking fingers to grasp and reposition the nylon, I felt the gurgling of an empty stomach; it's just that I wasn't hungry. I'd come to the diner—our favorite place—not to eat but because it was Friday afternoon and this was where I was supposed to be.

The previous five hundred or so Fridays had meant a day off work for me but, more importantly, a standing lunch date at Lydia's Diner for Patrick and me. It was our kick-start to the weekend, a tradition we both loved. But that was over now— no more club sandwiches or onion rings left to share with my husband. He was dead, and the greasy aroma of french fries and pot roast sandwiches did nothing but exacerbate the unwell feeling I suffered because of it.

"Waitingononemore?"Awaitress,surprisinglyunrecognizable, wore a familiar uniform and stood over me, a seasoned patron, perhaps a step too close. She tapped the nicked-here-and-there serving tray, anxious to scribble on her barely used order pad, its pale green background now reminding me of the decorative vases that had anchored my husband's casket just hours before.

Was I *waiting on one more?* The echoing words cut through me, and I wanted to correct her because there wasn't a one more for me. I was one less and, apparently, also empty of a response. Before I could find a way to say, "No, it's just me," or even, "No," which seems so simple now, Goldie came on the scene.

"Samantha, I thought I told you this was my section. Run along now."

"But I get tables one through five...," she whined, emphatic eyes fixed on the number-four-engrained plastic square glued to the table's edge, her voice doused with a hint of something that made me peg her as a know-it-all.

"I *said*, run along-g-g," Goldie seethed through a clenched jaw, neither worried nor uncomfortable over the fact that she wasn't technically the boss. She had, however, been working at Lydia's longer than I'd been eating there, so that had to count for something.

The two of us watched Samantha trot away and bust through the double doors leading to the kitchen, and even though Goldie and I both sort of smirked, she turned to me, her face now gentle and sincere.

"I'm so sorry, Julia. Patrick was a good man. Always smiling and so polite...treated us ladies around here like queens." She smiled. "And I know the two of you were very happy. Everyone could see that."

They were heartwarming words, but I fought a silent, erratic bouncing of my chest as I tried to catch my breath. She was right. We were happy—so happy.

My parents hadn't been able to attend the funeral, due to my father's poor health. Not having him there was difficult, but his Lou Gehrig's diagnosis was worse, and my "doting" mother refused to leave his side. I'd called home the night Patrick passed, asking Mom to put Dad on the line, but she refused, saying, "He's much too tired to speak, especially to you," and after her catty remark, she hung up the phone. I called again the next morning, knowing it was the day a home health nurse typically looked after Dad while Mom ran errands, but apparently they'd switched the schedule. *Just my luck.*

"Please put Dad on the line." My exhausted voice nearly broke as I begged, "I really need to speak to him."

"Anything you can tell him, you can tell me," she announced, identical to the many times I'd heard it since my early teen years. I could have lost my cool, spouted off an ill-delivered comment regarding the way some things never change, and told her to shut up and give the phone to Dad—the parent I actually loved—but I didn't have the energy. Instead, I broke into tears that I tried to conceal and said I'd call back later.

"Wait...Julia, wait!" I barely heard her shout just before my finger reached the end button.

I called back an hour later and, surprisingly, my father answered. "Hey doodlebug." My already broken heart shattered at the sound of his semi-slurred speech; I was crying again, nearly hyperventilating this time. When I'd calmed enough, he said, "Oh sweetie, tell me what's the matter."

"It's Patrick...," I began, still crying. "He's gone."

He stayed on the call for a while, and I told him everything. He wanted to fly in for the funeral, but I told him not to worry, that it would be too much of a hassle, too taxing of a trip. He insisted, but Mom left a voicemail later that night saying she was putting her foot down. They wouldn't be able to attend, and for once I agreed with her. There was no reason either of them should have to wrestle with Dad's wheelchair, and I knew public places were sometimes embarrassing for him.

"And...I'm sorry about Patrick," she added before saying good-bye. "I really am sorry."

Patrick was raised by a number of unfortunate foster families, and because he never regarded any of them as home, there were no relatives at his funeral. There was, however, a slew of coworkers and friends, people we'd grown close to over the past several years. They were the closest thing to family there could be, perhaps closer, and you could say they were the relatives we'd picked for ourselves. Goldie, our favorite waitress, was certainly one of them.

"I'm sorry, dear, didn't mean to get you all upset," she said, sliding into the booth. She wrapped her arms around my heaving shoulders as if to steal some of the pain. A minute later, I raised my head from her shoulder, dabbing hopeless eyes. Couldn't I just close them and go to Patrick? I was only thirty-three, not many years in the grand scheme of things, but all of a sudden they felt like enough.

"That's my girl," Goldie said, rubbing my back. "What can I get you, dear? You must be famished."

"I'm not hungry."

"That's not gonna fly with me, missy." She stood and looked down her nose, reminding me that she'd always had a way of taking care of us.

"Fine. I'll take my usual shake."

"Now there's a start." She winked before following Samantha's path into the kitchen.

She emerged with a typically tall soda-shop glass filled with smooth, blended chocolate. As she scooted in next to me, I noticed the three extra cherries, no whipped cream, and how grateful I was to have her there. Samantha wouldn't have sat down at all, but if she had, she'd have sat across from me. But no, not Goldie—she knew to leave Patrick's side of the booth alone, and that's only the beginning of why she was never just my waitress.

TWO

Julia

MY LIFELONG STATUS as a daddy's girl would never appear on *48 Hours Mystery* or find its way onto a police station bulletin as a crime that needed solving. The motives and outcome regarding the relationship between my parents and me had long been crystal clear.

My mother was the mom my classmates thought highly of, the put-together woman their mothers likely envied. There wasn't a class party she didn't throw or a school dance she didn't make perfect. Our house was always spick-and-span, and on most nights, a made-from-scratch meal adorned our little dinner table. But those were only her outward traits, a picture to be seen.

Helen was some kind of perfectionist. I'd like to say it was obsessive-compulsive disorder, but even the worst symptoms of that always seemed too mild an explanation for her behavior. All I know is that I couldn't erase the years of abysmal memories her flawlessly folded linens failed to overwhelm.

Everyone probably thought our home was warm and lovely, that my mother nurtured me in the adoring way she did her extensive backyard garden. The people who thought that were wrong, but it wasn't their fault—how were they to know the things my mother said to me behind closed doors? They weren't in our car after the fourth grade Halloween party when she confiscated my candy, educating me—no, scolding me—on the importance of staying slim. No one else heard what I heard after the sixth grade winter wonderland dance: I participated too much during the fast songs, not enough during the others, but when one of the boys did ask me to slow dance, I stood too close to him and now everyone probably thinks I'm a slut.

Once a week, like some firm-faced Marine, she'd wear a white glove and trace her fingers over the bookshelves and nightstands in my room; if she found dust, I'd have to spend my television time—thirty minutes a night—and then some re-cleaning my room or, depending on the mood she was in, scrubbing toilets.

Yes, my mother was always an impeccable cook, but I often left the dinner table with a bad taste in my mouth. Daddy would say something that made me laugh, and I'd snort with a mouth full of food, or maybe, like any kid has done at least once, I'd accidentally knock over a glass of milk. Any little thing of the sort would send my mother into a full-blown passive-aggressive lecture.

"Julia, darling, were you raised in a barn? Are little girls supposed to snort like hogs at the dinner table?"

Although she'd said *darling* and her voice was calm, there was a cold calculation to the way she'd maintained unerring posture, holding her silverware like I imagine the Queen of England would. Lips taut, she'd glance my way, her haughty eyes full of dissatisfaction.

Opposites attract, that's what they say, and I have a theory that they started saying it the day my parents wed. My father, I could tell, was never impressed with the way my mother chose to treat me, but I think he subscribed to an old-school notion that parenting should be left up to the mother and breadwinning to the father. He never shirked his responsibilities there, and even though every ounce of parental comfort I knew came from him, I wish he would've stood up for me more often. I spent years waiting for the day he'd draw a line in the sand and say enough is enough, and it finally came toward the end of my senior year of high school.

By then I was so shy and unsure of myself that I'm surprised I found the confidence to fill out a college application at all, let alone send it thousands of miles from home. I was accepted, and I'll never forget the moment I found out, how my mother stormed into the living room where I was doing homework. Waving the opened acceptance letter in the air, she shrieked, "What's this?! Julia, tell me you did not apply to this school...it was *not* on the list!"

The list. Oh God, the list. Her choices, in her penmanship, had been hanging on the refrigerator since the start of tenth grade.

Thank heaven my father came home from work early that day or else I probably would have apologized and promised to attend a school closer to Connecticut.

"Helen," my father boomed, low and steady, setting his briefcase on the coffee table. "Julia will attend the school of her choosing, and *you* will have nothing to do with it."

Oh, the bewilderment in my mother's eyes!

"I beg your pardon?" Her chin, tilted in disbelief, seemed not to have thoroughly received the message that a new day had come.

Daddy stared back at her, not flinching a centimeter, meaning, with every ounce of him, what he'd said.

"This," Mother Helen squawked, "is absolutely unacceptable! She didn't have permission!"

My father took three giant steps forward and grabbed her flailing arm, jerking it down to her side.

"*This,*" he said, looking at the twice-folded letter, which had fallen to the ground, "has nothing to do with you, am I clear?"

I thought she might spit in his face, but she instead averted her attention to her arm, seeming to remember the rule written on the same scroll as Daddy's parenting style: The husband's opinion stands. Once again, through gritted teeth, he asked, "Am. I. Clear?"

She nodded reluctantly, yanked her arm away from his firm grasp, and marched off to the kitchen to start dinner. We had meatloaf, mashed potatoes, and green beans that night, and Daddy and I conversed delightfully over the basket of dinner rolls as if my mother weren't even there.

Six months later, I packed my belongings and prepared for a new life as a college student in San Diego. "I've always wanted to see the California coast. Now I have an excuse," Daddy had said, but Mother didn't see it that way.

The night before I left, she slipped into my room long after I'd gone to sleep. She was drunk, for the first time I'd ever seen, and lay on the bed, curled up at my side as she pleaded, "Don't leave, Julia...don't abandon me...you can't do this...I have nothing left... what will I do with myself?" Hot tears raced down my cheeks, and as she lay there on the verge of passing out, I thought of changing my plans. But before I could work out the logistics, she caught a spurt of energy and reminded me why I'd longed to move so far away in the first place. Staggering around the room, she finally paused and pointed at a picture of me from the fifth grade.

"You were a little chubby back then...not as smart as I'd hoped." She turned to me, my tear-filled eyes stinging as I observed her pouting lower lip. I rose from the bed and led her out onto the living room couch, laying a blanket over her abdomen as I reasoned there was no sense waking my dad to explain it. She could do that on her own in the morning; I was going back to bed.

"Horrible!" she shouted, causing me to stop in the middle of the hallway and turn my ear toward her. "I'm a horrible mother," she whispered, and for a short minute that somehow felt too long, I listened to her sob until she fell asleep. I returned to my room but, an hour later, woke to the sound of dry heaving coming from the adjacent bathroom. I shuffled across the hall and plugged in a night light near the bathroom sink, asking my toilet-hugging mother if she needed anything. I knew she was still drunk, but the look in her eye as she told me, "Go away! I hate you, just leave...I hate you!" seemed more real than any other thing she'd ever said to me.

Four years passed, and our relationship carried on about the same as ever. She sent care packages filled to the brim with homemade goods, newly released novels, and little gadgets for my apartment kitchen, but when I called home, her words were full of mixed messages. She'd say things that made me feel guilty for being so far away but, in the same breath, acted like life was better without me there. "I'm telling you, Julia, this empty nest thing is a phenomenon...best thing to ever happen to your father and me...I feel like a brand new woman, like I've been set free."

I graduated and decided to take a job in Chicago, and for weeks leading up to the big move, she'd call and harass me: "Are you trying to kill your father and I? Do you just absolutely detest us? Don't you think we deserve to have our only child back home? What if we die? Won't you feel bad then, Julia?"

I tried my best to assure her my decision had nothing to do with them, that I didn't hate them, and that moving to Chicago for this job would be a great experience for me.

"Ohhh. I see," she'd said in a leading tone.

"What?"

"Julia, you're a lesbian, aren't you? Oh my God, Richard, she's a lesbian! We'll never be able to show our faces in public again!"

"Mom! Good grief, I never said that."

"Yes you did."

"No, I most certainly did not!"

"Don't yell at me, young lady!"

And that was the conversation that made me believe in aliens. It was the only explanation. Martians had implanted a rare, creature-from-another-planet microchip into my mother's brain and eaten her heart for breakfast, and it must have happened years ago, probably before I was even born.

I swear it was divine intervention when Patrick and I met just two weeks after my move to Chicago. The change machine at our then local Coin N Clean was broken, and as I switched my whites from washer to dryer, he walked over and asked if I had change for a dollar. I scrounged four quarters from the bottom of my purse and that was that. We became inseparable.

It's ironic, I suppose, that I was folding his undershirts when our love story reached a shocking end. It was almost seven o'clock on a wintery Monday evening, and I was waiting for Patrick to get home from work. I'd called earlier to ask if he would stop and buy ricotta cheese on his way. I'd been a little nervous to ask, not because of my habitual ability to forget at least one thing on the grocery list but because he'd been in a weird mood. I knew it was a busy time at work and didn't want to inconvenience him, but he was unbothered by my request, chipper even.

"Oh, you're making lasagna for dinner? I'll get some wine too...the kind we had last time, what was it called?"

"I don't know, Mollie's or something. It was a merlot, that I do know." I was tempted to add an assurance that it really was fine if he didn't have time to pick up the wine, but I knew the convenience store, Johnny's Liquor, Etc., was on his way home and there was a pretty good chance he already planned to stop for his almost daily wind-down ritual of Diet Pepsi and a handful of scratch-off lottery tickets.

"Okay honey, be back around six...six thirty at the very latest," he'd promised.

"See you then, babe."

There was a knock and the doorbell rang, and I sort of rolled my eyes, smiling as I shut the dryer door and breezed out of the laundry room, thinking this was another one of Patrick's silly gestures. I thought I'd open the front door to find him holding a bouquet of flowers or belting a cheesy love song, claiming to work for one of those singing telegram companies. But I couldn't have been more wrong.

The police officer confirmed my name and told me there'd been an incident. "I'm very sorry, ma'am," he said, "but your husband was shot this evening."

In an armed robbery gone sideways, he'd found himself in the middle of liquor store crossfire. Ambulances were called to the scene, but by the time they reached emergency room doors,

Patrick was gone.

The officer drove me to the hospital, and there, in a small, private room, I sobbed over my husband's lifeless body, my mind spinning as I took in all I'd lost and just how quickly. His light-blue button-up shirt had been torn open by the paramedics, that I could tell from the buttons, but there on the cuff were deep-purple splatters of Miley's Merlot, and I screamed, imagining Patrick's last living seconds.

We'd planned to start trying for a baby the following month. We were thinking of buying a larger home. We'd always talked about seeing Cape Cod in the fall, Hawaii in the spring. Ten years we'd been together, nine of them married, and all of a sudden, we were no more—thanks to a nineteen-year-old thug who got away with thirty-seven dollars, my husband's life, and every hope I'd ever had for the future.

THREE

Adrian

I CALLED OUT for Dominic and closed the warehouse door behind me, realizing I'd interrupted him in the middle of a chew-out. One of the new guys was on his ninth life for miscounting cartons of hot merchandise. Dom, my right-hand man, made his point and ended the conversation before strutting over to me. He had this admirable, quiet confidence, and at the end of the day, I needed someone competent and smooth, but not a snake, and Dom was always that guy.

"What can I do for ya, boss?"

He called me boss sometimes, but only in front of our younger guys, just to help establish a certain respect, a pecking order, if you will. I never asked him to; he just did it. Dom and I were friends, brothers really. We'd seen some hoopla in our day—real urban-cowboy type stuff. Anyway, we saved each other's haunches more than a few times. I command and demand respect, as anyone in my position would, but having Dom's respect meant more knowing he had mine.

"It's time for the meeting."

"Now?" he asked, surprised.

"Now."

"But Adrian..."

"Yeah, I know, change of plans...we've got Mickey and Dale in thirty."

"Seriously?"

"Do I have to hold your hand or what?"

We took the rear exit and got in the car. Dom drove, and once we were on the road, he and I rehearsed, in our own language and with the music nearly blasting, what was about to go down. We'd been making friends with Mickey Santino, a guy tough enough to be a gangster but not smart enough to be good at it. He belonged to the same crime family, but he didn't work for me. It's sort of a third-cousin kind of thing; his boss reported to my boss.

Anyway, Mickey and I had had a not-so-friendly rivalry going on for years, but now it was time to start fresh. I wasn't doing it to be nice; I was doing it to make a score. I'd always known how to play Mickey—he was as ill-prepared as he was ugly—and I just knew I could get what I needed from him and make him look pathetic in the process. He should have known I was making a play, but, unsurprisingly, he was two steps behind.

I could have pulled the score off without him, but it would be better to get Mickey on board, so I overlooked the pain associated with simply being in his presence. It all started a few weeks prior to this meeting, when I attended a party thrown by one of my bosses. It was a big deal—a huge house shindig with caterers and girls and pretty much anything else a man might want. Dom and I ran into Holly Gadaldi, this girl he knew from high school. She was working the party to earn quick bucks and, not only that, turned out she was Mickey's cousin on his mother's side. Insert eye roll here.

I was just about to step away from the conversation when Holly mentioned that she also worked as a maid for this guy named Charles Ainsley. The reason it caught my attention was because everyone in Chicago knew the Ainsley name. They had more money than any human would know what to do with—I mean richer than rich—so I stuck around a while longer, gave Holly some compliments, and largely overtipped when she brought me a drink. I got Holly's number; we flirted a little; and then I enjoyed the rest of the evening thinking I'd just planted a pretty good seed.

So, not even two days later, I met this guy—Roger. He'd come to my strip club, Fancy's, to update our security system, and he and I started chewing the fat. Seemed like he really knew his stuff, so I asked him how long he'd been doing this. "A while," he said and went on to tell me he had some pretty big accounts in the area.

"Oh yeah, like who?" I asked.

He started rattling them off, and I salivated when he mentioned the Ainsley estate.

I asked and he started telling me stories about this Mr. Ainsley and the unusual collections he kept—mostly weird tribal art and stuff, but that's not all. Apparently the guy had acquired a rare jewelry collection from his recently dead uncle. It was worth millions and, come to find out, ole Charles Ainsley called Roger—my security system guy, by fate alone—to come over and set up a custom, secure wall display for the gems.

I could hardly believe my good fortune, and then, to make matters even more appealing, turned out this guy Roger was a Gadaldi—Holly Gadaldi's cousin on the other side! She was the one who referred Ainsley to him in the first place. At this point, I realized I was destined to make a score, so when Roger was done working, I set him up with a free meal and complimentary lap dance from one of our best girls. Roger and I were now pals; Holly and I were now seeing each other; and Charles Ainsley should have warmed up his writing hand—he was about to learn, if he hadn't already, that police reports and insurance claims exist primarily at length.

The reason I needed Mickey to think he was in on this was because the last thing I needed was for him to tell Holly I'm no good. I needed her and Roger more than I needed anyone in this entire scheme, so there was nothing I wouldn't do to prevent scaring them away. So, although I hated every second, I started getting chummy with ole Mickey Mouse. I'd done him a favor here and there, nothing too over the top until I stumbled upon a quick-fix situation that saved him from a problem that could have sent him away.

I'd done the preparations, had the schmuck thinking we'd forged somewhat of an alliance and that the future only meant deeper pockets for the both of us. But most importantly, Mickey was now in my debt and he knew it. I told him I needed to talk to him and had a birdie sing him a little tune called "Ole Adrian's Planning Something Huge," and bing-bam-boom, suddenly we were having a meeting, and not only that but Mickey pushed it up by twelve hours.

I usually preferred public appearances to take place on my terms, but I figured it wouldn't hurt to mix things up a bit. Variety is the spice of life, it's just that I wouldn't know, because I'd been sitting at the same table at Lydia's Diner for almost fifteen years now, and I have to be honest and say that when Dom and I walked in to see Mickey and his new lapdog, Dale, in my spot like they owned the place, I literally felt like killing them both.

"Gentlemen," I said, holding my arms out to adjust the sleeves of my suit jacket. We were all in suits, but Dale and Mickey looked as cheap as ever, which shouldn't have surprised me, because Mickey always had a cheesy sense of style—that and he was a chintzy bastard.

Like a toddler unknowing of his place, Dale was first to speak, making a comment about our waitress being sex on a stick—"Hey, A, check her out," he added—and just the disgusting way he said it, like he had some kind of a real chance with her, went right through me. I called him by the wrong name to let him know just how little he mattered and made it clear that he could call me Mr. De Luca. His boss, Mickey, however, was someone I'd known a long time, I said, someone with whom I "share a mutual respect" (or some bull like that), respect he might consider showing our waitress.

Dale shook his head that he understood and took a feminine sip of his ice water with lemon and lime. *What kind of man asks for a goddamn lime?*

I must have flattered Mickey with that "mutual respect" bologna, because he didn't seem to have a problem with me ripping into his little underling. Perhaps he was too focused on the numbers we might share, too curious to find out what I might need from him, to care about anything else.

"So I hear there's something big going down," he said.

"You might've heard right," I said.

"So what is it?" He was practically drooling already.

"Do you want in or not?"

"I need to know details first."

"No you don't. You either want in or you don't."

He hesitated but smiled. "Oh, I want in."

"Well now, that was a good decision, because it's a million-dollar score." So I fudged the numbers a tad.

"Okay, when? What are we doing?"

"Calm down...just calm down. No need to rush ahead."

"We only came to see if you wanted in," Dom admitted. "There's more to come when the time is right."

It was obvious that Mickey was chomping at the bit with curiosity, but overall everyone was satisfied, and the conversation became more casual. Thank God Dom was in a chatty mood, because I just couldn't stomach more of the small "let's all be best friends" talk. Calm and silent but thinking about my many irons in the fire, I went to work on a plate of open-faced roast beef, my mind wandering to the times and places I'd strike.

Somewhere in the middle of Mickey's brainless, dry story about his recent trip to Miami, I came to, out of my daydream, and realized I was grinning. As for the reason, no one could have been more shocked than me. I'd looked up from the table just in time to see her walk through the door, and from the second I laid eyes on her, I knew I had to have her.

We finished the meal; our new partners left; and Dom went to the car at my request. There was a new deal to close, one I wouldn't need his help with.

FOUR

Julia

I SAID I wouldn't, but just one week after the funeral, I found myself following through on our weekly tradition of Friday lunch at Lydia's. It just seemed right. Or did it? I wasn't sure. I'd been feeling so much of everything and nothing that I needed more time to sort through my life, which I suppose is natural for a newly minted widow.

Widow—what an astonishing thing to be and a startling thing to feel so early in life. Patrick liked to joke about the types of men I'd surely come across in the nursing home. "You'll marry the one with the most hair, I just know it," he would say, making me laugh every time, because Patrick's hairline was beginning to thin and retreat. He was self-conscious, so I denied noticing it over and over again.

"I'll marry the rich one," I'd say, trying to change the subject.

"First husband for love, second for money, eh?" he once replied.

"Technically you make more money than me."

"But you married me because of love...right?"

"Hmmm..." I scrunched my nose, pretending to think it over until he came after me.

"You greedy...little...gold digger!" he yelled, joking of course, both of us on the floor as he smothered and tickled me.

But now I sat in our booth merely dreaming of our jokes, my smile fading into nothing as it occurred to me how unfair it was that the tickling had made me so happy. No one told us how wrong the laughter would later seem, that the time between premature baldness and widow was shorter than we could ever guess.

I thought about what it was like in the beginning, how in love we were from day one. My eyes never strayed from him; my imagination never ran with the thought of having another, and from everything I could assume, neither had Patrick's. I knew we were forever, death being the only thing that would ever separate us; it's just that when I thought of the end, I'd always imagined it happening so much later in life, with the nursing home scenario we'd joked about. Maybe a few times I had wondered to myself what I'd do if Patrick ran around on me or passed away at an early age. I didn't think either of them likely, but even still, I viewed him as my only one—ever. And as I sat at that table waiting for Goldie to bring my lunch, everything inside me reiterated what I'd always believed: I'd never want anyone else.

In the nine days since Patrick's death, well-meaning friends had made comments about how young I was and how much I had to offer, presumably to another man, which I thought disgusting and insensitive of them to say. Maybe that's what some women would have wanted to hear—that they'd find love again, that there was still time. Maybe some would want to be coddled and encouraged in this way, but I didn't. No, I wanted to be comforted for the sheer fact that the love of my life was taken from me in an instant, brutal way, murdered in a piece-of-crap liquor store, and there wasn't an eligible bachelor that could ever be appealing or interested in me enough to make that loss go away.

Go away—that's what I wanted to say to the man who, out of nowhere, walked up to *our* booth and stood next to me. I barely looked at him, gave him nothing more than a peripheral glance until he finally spoke.

"Lovely day, isn't it?"

Are you kidding me?

"Mind if I join you?"

Where's Goldie? Please, God, send him away.

He took a step, and just as he began to sit down opposite me—in Patrick's place—I perked up. "Yes, I do mind...I mind very much."

"That I sit with you?"

I nodded in the affirmative, suddenly nervous as I studied him for the first real time. He was well dressed, quite handsome (I noticed but didn't register), and I could tell, from voice alone, that he was from New York. Or at least that was my best guess, according to the way he sounded so much like my Long Island-hailing coworker, Jennifer. I'd never been good with accents, whether it be identifying or impersonating them, but this time, I'd have put money on it.

He froze, caught between standing and sitting until he took one giant step away from the booth and returned himself upright.

"I'm sorry, have I offended you?"

Embarrassed yet unapologetic, I asked him to leave.

"Okay," he said, seeming to mean it truly was all right.

The man turned and walked out the door, and as I listened to the bells jingle and chime against the glass, the fact that he was gone very much occurred to me, and I felt nothing but a loneliness even emptier than I'd experienced just half a minute before.

FIVE

Adrian

MICKEY WAS GETTING Holly on board, and aside from that, everything was business as usual for a few days—usual except for the fact that I couldn't stop thinking about my failure with the girl at the diner. There was something there, a compulsion to talk to her, win her over, maybe introduce her to my sheets—not so hard for a guy like me, and I'd had plenty of practice.

What can I say? I had a good face and a clever tongue, and maybe it helped that I knew how to use it. Plus, there was the money. Granted, my life was—well, let's go with untraditional. It was challenging, yes, but it was a good life that brought me happiness, and the ladies flocked to me like dogs to a barbecue.

But this particular woman was different, that I knew

immediately. She sailed into the diner as if she was coming home at the end of a particularly annoying day, and although this seemed to be a relief to her, there was something weighing her down. I'd overwhelm whatever it was or I'd fix it, one of the two, or maybe even both is what I was thinking, because if there's anything I was competent at, it was bullying and fixing. Most people interpret obstacles as a deterrent, but I saw opportunity, because walls often hide valuables, a prize to be won, and in this instance, I looked forward to the challenge of cracking away at this girl's shell.

At first it was a turn-on that she wanted nothing to do with me—typical male thing, I guess, always wanting what we can't have, valuing the struggle and the reward. But when she finally looked at me, when her eyes desperately pleaded that I not sit down, I surrendered. And surrendering ain't my thing.

"Please leave me alone," she'd said, and in that instant, there was nothing I wanted more than to do what she'd asked. Something about the way she had no energy to say anything more than those four words made me feel like such a jackass. And maybe on every other day of my life, walking out of that diner without the girl would have rattled the ole ego a bit, but on this day, I could only think of her—still was days later.

So I went back to Lydia's, hoping, on a stroke of pure luck, to see the girl again, but she wasn't there. I popped a squat at the counter and ordered a black coffee among the lunch crowd. Feeling a hand on my shoulder, I turned to see my Goldie, best-ever waitress that had once served meals to me on the night shift. Good for her for snagging more sensible hours, but hell, I missed seeing her.

"There's my girl."

"To what do I owe the pleasure of seeing the sun shine on

your face twice in one week now?" She asked it playfully but with suspicion.

"What's a man gotta do to snag some jitter juice without an interrogation around here?"

"Oh shush."

I liked that Goldie was her kooky, sassy self with me, that she knew exactly who I was and the types of things my family was responsible for, and yet she didn't hold back. And in my world, this lifestyle that demands a sharp, constant stream of mental awareness and mind games so tricky you're not sure which handprint is your own, it's good to just be known. It's nice to hear "Merry Christmas" and not wonder if the person means, "Merry Christmas, enjoy it...you'll be dead by New Year's." It's refreshing to hear that your breath is not so fresh, and Goldie had proven herself perfectly capable of bringing this type of thing to my attention.

But maybe the most important piece of information she ever gave to me came when I asked about the girl in the booth. "She was sitting in that one over there." I pointed, and although she followed my gaze, she didn't seem too keen on participating in my game of detective.

"You honestly expect me to know who you're talking about?" She was playing coy, and she knew I knew.

"Blonde hair... cute frame... permanent melancholy expression."

"Lotta people come through here, Adrian."

"Come on, it was Friday," I said as she turned away. I thought maybe she wouldn't come back, but she waltzed around to the service side of the bar and leaned in to face me, forearms extended on the counter. Honestly, I wasn't sure what she'd say, but I noticed the deep lines extending from her eyes and wondered if she ever worried about me.

"That sweet little woman's been coming here for the past ten years."

"Then why haven't I ever seen her?"

"Because she eats at regular times like a normal person and you're lucky if you eat dinner by midnight, that's why."

Goldie was right, and I gave her an admitting smirk for it. "So when will she be back?"

"Probably never."

"Oh, come on. Don't tell me she's been coming here for a decade and now all a sudden, because I'm asking, act like she's moved or something."

"Why *are* you asking?"

"I took a shine to her, that's all."

"She's a good one, I'll say that." And then she started brewing coffee as if she'd suddenly run out of words for the day. It was irritating, not just because she wouldn't tell me what I wanted to know but also because here, all this time, I'd been thinking I was her favorite, that if anyone came sniffing around asking personal questions about me, she'd keep it all under lock and key. But apparently there was competition.

"Hey Goldie, remember that time I spotted the meter maid at your windshield and he somehow ended up with a broken nose that made him forget about the ticket in his hand?"

"Don't be an idiot, just zip it and drink your coffee."

"I won't leave you alone until you tell me about her, and we both know how annoying I can be."

"Yes. Yes we do." She sighed, standing directly in front of me again. "Now listen here. The girl you're referring to is not some hot little conquest next on your list."

"I would never." I winked, gently raising my hands as if under arrest.

"Hush, I'm not done. I can see why you'd be interested in her. She's a pretty thing...sweet as she is funny...loyal. Very, very loyal..." She trailed off, nodding her head ever so slightly and controlled.

"So what's the problem?"

"She's not some moody, dark-minded loner like you might think. And don't think I didn't notice you moving in on her last week...like a dirty ole dog..."

"Whoa, Goldie." I chuckled, but she didn't see the humor.

"Listen...leave her alone. That look on her face, what did you call it, permanent melancholy? You're a moron."

"So enlighten me."

"She comes in here for lunch every Friday with her husband... until recently...because he's dead. So the woman you met a few days ago is not the same Julia I've known, and she can come in here wearing whatever kinda look she wants for as long as she needs...until she's herself again."

Surprised, I asked, "Do you think that will ever happen?"

"Do you?" She wore a knowing look and left to meet a customer at the register.

Probably not, I thought but wanted the chance to find out.

SIX

Julia

ANOTHER WEEK FLEW by, except it dragged on in a way that made me wonder if I'd ever reach a stage of equilibrium somewhere in the neighborhood of normal. I missed Patrick with an all-encompassing pain that never left yet had a way of sneaking up on me. I'd sworn off lasagna and wine, even bought new underwear when the clean ones ran out, but I was eventually forced to open the laundry room door and meet the ghosts living in the place I'd been just moments before my life came crashing down. I shrieked and cried at the hospital that night and sobbed myself to sleep, and the memory of that, the soundtrack to the worst thing I could have imagined happening, played on repeat no matter what I was thinking about.

I saw Patrick in every glance and felt him everywhere. I'd tie my tennis shoes and think of the way he explained the proper lacing technique, not just to me but to everyone, so it seemed. He was right that his way prevents blisters, but the over-the-top need he felt to educate our friends and neighbors was the one way Patrick could really embarrass me in public. The thought of it now made me laugh, in much the same way our living room rug sent my heart into a sad, sad spiral, remembering the day we picked it out. I was sitting on the edge of a showroom couch, leaning over to inspect a rug I liked but wasn't so sure about.

"I don't know...," I said. "It's got...those swirly things, what are they called?"

"Swirly things?" Patrick asked as he sat next to me. "Are swirly things really so bad?"

"I don't know, that's what I'm asking you." Home decor was neither my worst nor my strongest attribute, and I was past due to eat, so suffice it to say, my impatience was growing.

"Okay then, let's test it out," he said, and before I could understand what he meant, he pushed me over, and we toppled onto a sea of swirly things. I slapped his shoulder, but it didn't stop him from bear-hugging me and rolling us three times over. Why was he always tackling me? My first inclination of annoyance and embarrassment was soon stifled by this troubling thought: *I'm acting like my mother.* So I forced myself to let out an entertained giggle and gave my husband an eyes-sparkling smile and a kiss on the cheek before unlatching myself. Catching my breath, I rose to my feet, straightened my clothing, and retied my ponytail.

"Paisley. That's what they're called," I said.

"And are we a fan of paisley?"

"I believe so," I answered, knowing the shy grin I wore to be completely real.

But nothing about his absence from my life seemed real, and I began to measure time in trips to Lydia's. I couldn't wait for, yet dreaded, each approaching Friday. I wanted to be in our booth and feel his presence in the same way and for the same reasons I wore his T-shirts to bed: to be where he had been and touch the things he'd touched, to experience any last whiff of him I could. But no matter how well it started out, it always ended the same: without him.

I'd been without him for two weeks, and I walked into Lydia's Diner prepared to spend lunch—with the exception of Goldie—alone. But that didn't exactly happen, and it took me a while to decide how I felt about it.

Adrian

I should've just left her alone, like someone with a real heart. It would have saved me a lot of trouble in the end, not to mention with Goldie. The woman smacked me upside the head when she saw me come strolling into the diner just days after we'd had our chat about the mystery girl.

"Friday, quarter to twelve, third time I've seen you this week. Don't tell me it's a coincidence," she'd said.

But I sat down anyway, because even though I felt like a real snake, I'd left the diner a few days before and gone home only to decide that I had to come back. I wanted to see Julia again. I went from wanting a roll in the hay with her to wanting to help her, and although I really didn't know how or why I thought I had the power to do that, I decided I should at least be her friend. And maybe I did want something more with her, but I also felt a need to fix her, to absorb her pain.

So I chose the booth across from where I thought she'd sit, and when she came in, when she sat down and very obviously ignored or didn't notice my existence, I started doubting my chances. I knew a thing or two about loss, sure, but she didn't know that, and this wasn't about me.

"Adrian," I said bluntly, curious what she'd say in response, which turned out to be absolutely nothing. So again, without request, I announced my name, but this time I turned my body toward her and patiently waited. A few seconds passed, and it was like the echo of what I'd said stole her attention. Politely, she looked at me, then over her shoulder, and back to me again. I watched her eyes scan the general area and it was like she was making sure I wasn't talking to someone else. I wasn't, and in that moment, as she suddenly appeared to feel some kind of rude, I glimpsed into her precious little soul.

"I'm sorry...what?" she asked.

"You didn't ask, but my name is Adrian," I said, stretching out my hand with an assertiveness that normally worked, but perhaps my confidence was better suited for a nightclub.

Without missing a beat, she reached across the aisle to shake my hand, and as her eyes met mine, I knew she recognized me from the last time I tried talking to her. "Hi, Adrian. You're right, I didn't ask." And with that, she returned to facing exactly forward. Ouch—but good, I like a little sass.

"The polite thing now," I said "is for you to tell me your name." I tried to say it playfully, without pressure, and maybe it helped that I already knew her name, but it didn't matter. She wasn't amused.

"Can you not see that I'm married?" She held up her left ring finger as if she were flipping me off, and as much as I wanted to counter, "No, you're not," I knew that was a lie. Her husband was dead, but she was still married to him, and even though my intentions were good, I was crossing a line.

I glanced at the stone and, after immediately thinking it too small to give the woman you're hoping will love you all her life, wondered what Julia's late husband did for a living. It was probably something noble, something parents all over America would be happy to brag about and, at the same time, an average existence, no doubt.

But who was I to judge existences? I had more than a run-of-the-mill existence, a few loyal friends, and the sort of power that can make a man wealthy. But most, if not all, would say that how I made a living was anything but noble. I had influence and the fruits of hard, smart labor, but that didn't mean I slept well. Peace of mind often escaped me, and even before Julia slipped away to sit at the counter, I knew she and her husband had something I'd always wanted but had never gotten around to prioritizing. I say that like love is a goal to achieve, a thing a person really has some kind of control over. I don't know, maybe you can control it. You can at least invite yourself to it, but I never had.

I was engaged once—loved her, but I wasn't in love. Now there's a story we've all heard more times than we can count—all of us except Marla.

She had a body like you wouldn't believe. She understood my life, maybe even got off on it a little more than what was required. She had every check in the box, and she knew it. We were out shopping one day and went into a jewelry store, I thought to buy a bracelet or bauble for our two-year anniversary, but we walked out with a three-and-a-half-carat diamond ring she started wearing on a significant finger. A week later she was hounding me about an engagement party.

"Should we throw it as soon as possible or give ourselves time to really do it up big?"

"I don't want to," I said.

"You don't want to make it a big deal?"

"Marla..."

"Do you even want this party, or do I have to do all the work?"

"I don't want to get married." I cut right to it, which barely made me sad, but Marla shot off the ceiling.

"Then why did you ask?!"

"I didn't." And that was the truth. Marla was legit, a real great girl. But she asked to keep the ring, which was fine with me, and now I rarely think about her.

Love is curious.

Powerful.

All-encompassing.

Confusing.

Once found, love—true love—is conclusive, irrevocable. *But Adrian*, you might say. *Love ends all the time. Divorce kills more marriages than death.*

Have you ever thought about divorced people? Really wondered about them? I think they cry for a while and move on with life, yes. Sometimes they find someone else, and maybe that situation is better than before; maybe it's not. But I think they wonder what their previous other half is doing. Maybe they hope the other person is happy; maybe they don't. Doesn't matter, because they're still hoping for something. And if they're not, well, I'd say they were never really in love in the first place.

I could be a hard man. I'd done things that slowly, and then all at once, chipped away at my humanness. Certain parts of my soul were barren, numb from the images I'd seen and created. But just like every other man, average existence or not, my desires were primal. I required food and water, but what I really needed was a battle to wage and a beauty to love—a love so intense that if it all came crashing down, I'd spend every moment to myself in one of two ways: wishing her well, because I loved her so much; or wishing her misery, because I loved her so much.

I'd spent my whole life waiting for the person I'd either die for or want dead, and that sad little widow was the one. I watched her from across the diner; her back was to me, but I could see the way she hovered the fork over her plate, how she waited to put food on it until after she finished the previous bite. When she leaned over to pick her purse up off the floor, I peeped the bare skin of her lower back with a glance long enough to wonder if she was one of those women who buy their clothes a size too big or if the grief had stolen the pounds. Knowing the answer, I stood and walked out the door, its bells seeming to jingle a dismal tune.

SEVEN

Adrian

ONE WEEK LATER, I pulled the same trick and showed up at Lydia's because I knew Julia would be there. Things at work were really heating up, so truthfully, I didn't have the time to spare, but I knew it'd be worth it. I figured she'd keep up the game of snubbing me for a while, and who would blame her? But I didn't really care when she'd warm up. I just wanted to see her.

I arrived mere minutes before Julia, and when she walked in and turned the corner only to see me sitting there again, she just sort of stopped and stared at me. At first she looked scared, like maybe she was beginning to process these instances as danger instead of a nuisance, but all at once she relaxed and started walking again. Like a moody teen, she tossed her purse into the booth and sat down. She was slightly pissed, and this of course made the afternoon all the more exciting to me.

"Hey, how ya doin'?" I asked, as if we were old classmates or coworkers, something chummy.

"Fine," she said, without making eye contact, and looked into the menu like she was honestly reading it, like I didn't know she had it memorized. I nodded and went about my business, dumping sugar into my coffee even though I'd always taken it black, and it must have really bugged her that she was being impolite because, within the minute, she looked my way and forced herself to reply, "And how are you?"

"I'm well. Thanks for asking." And I said it with a grin, because she seemed to be squirming inside. It was cute, and I think she was torn over whether she wanted me to shut up or keep talking, so I kept talking until Goldie came to take both orders and whisper to me that she was going to spit in mine. God, I loved that woman.

Julia warmed up to me little by little, but there was still an element of succinctness to her answers, and very rarely did she wander from letting me carry the conversation. I was making headway, and that was fun, but the fact that I hadn't discussed such normal things in quite a while, maybe ever, wasn't lost on me.

I learned Julia was a sixth grade teacher, and although that made sense based on everything I'd observed about her, it didn't explain why she was out to lunch in the middle of a school day.

"Private school. No class on Fridays...it's home learning."

"Home learning?"

"The parents get to decide the subject matter. Most of them use it as a day for museums and special trips. It's pretty cool."

With squinting eyes, I nodded along like I could actually imagine my parents taking me on a weekly field trip and coming up with their own curriculum. I guess, in a lot of ways, my dad had given me an education; I'd just never thought of it in such a structured way. The man never stepped foot in a museum, but he taught me real, useful things that can't be acquired by sitting at a desk but rather in the basements and back rooms of New York City.

"Special trips..." I let out a whistle and could tell she wasn't clear on whether I was impressed or thought the whole thing ridiculously over the top, and to be honest, neither was I.

"What do you do?" she asked.

"I'm a businessman." Technically not a lie, but she seemed to believe me. I was certainly dressed for it, maybe overdressed according to some standards, but I don't really do standards, and like my mother used to say, perhaps while fluffing her mink stole in preparation for the grocery store, "Better to be overdressed than underdressed," and I would have to agree.

My pocket was buzzing and our plates near empty, and although I didn't want to, I knew it was time to leave, so I told her I had to get going. "But I hope to see you again."

"Thank you," she said, "but I don't...I don't think..."

"Julia?" I was standing in the aisle now, looking at her warmly, naturally, thinking about how pretty she was even with the smearing of fear and grief she wore from head to toe.

She didn't say anything, just looked at me as if she might cry. I think there was some guilt there, like maybe she wanted to see me again too, if only to share another lunch across the aisle, but she knew she was supposed to be something else: alone.

"It's okay," I said, and a single tear fell down her cheek.

"What?" she asked.

"All of it." I gave her a gentle smile and walked to the counter to pay for both our meals. Exiting, I turned, happy over the fact she was already looking at me, and gave her a wink over my shoulder.

Julia

"I hope he's not bothering you, sweetie," Goldie said to me before I left to go home. "You need to tell me if he bothers you."

"No, it's fine."

"You sure? Because I can make him sit somewhere else. Better yet, I'll make him leave."

"It's fine, really."

"I know you're going through a hard time, Julia..." She trailed off, being careful with her words. "But someday...you might be up for...you know, a new life."

"Oh, I'm not interested in him."

"Well...good."

"Why? Why is that good?" I piped up. "What's wrong with him?"

"Oh, honey...I didn't mean it like that. He's a good guy...well, one of my favorites, to tell you the truth. But he's...a ladies' man, that's all. His life is complicated. You deserve better."

"Better?"

"Just more. You deserve more."

"Is this where you tell me I'm too good for him? Because I've never really agreed with that phrase." I was starting to get defensive for reasons I couldn't name.

"No, Julia. Well...yes. This is that part. You need someone different. Someone like Patrick was. Someone that will be home for dinner...stable...traditional."

"It doesn't even matter, because I'm not ready, but thanks

Goldie." I stood from the booth and gave her a hug. "See you next week."

"Take care, darlin'." She squeezed back.

I did a few errands, went home, and mostly forgot about Adrian, because there was a stack of book reports to grade and days' worth of lessons to plan by Monday, not to mention the approaching week full of special programming and time-consuming projects for which I still needed to prepare. But I caught my mind drifting to him later in the week, and by Wednesday, I was really starting to look forward to Friday's lunch.

I figured he'd be at Lydia's, like he'd been the previous three Fridays, but he wasn't. I assumed he was running late, until Goldie, looking reluctant, set a piece of order-pad paper in front of me. It was a note from Adrian, in his handwriting: *Last-minute trip out of town. See you next week.*

"I don't know why he'd feel the need to write this." I acted unimpressed, but on the inside, I was beaming.

"Mm-hmm." Goldie rolled her eyes and walked away, and I sat there feeling a slight giddiness that soon wore off and left me feeling bored.

I didn't move from the couch the next day except to fix pancakes and several bowls of popcorn that provided the little sustenance needed to make it through four movies. Halfway into the third, I got a text—*Excited to see you tonight! So pumped for GNO!*—from Nina, an old college friend. She'd emailed earlier in the week to say she would be in town for a work thing and suggested we meet up.

But now I didn't want to go, not in the slightest, and wondered why I'd made plans with her to begin with. We'd stayed in touch through the years, enough that she'd been invited to my wedding but not so much that it would be worth spending recent-college-grad income on a flight into town. As far as I knew, she had no idea Patrick had died, and for whatever reason, I didn't mention it in the email. Where would I have put it? Should I have sandwiched it between *Hi Nina, would love to meet up with you Saturday night* and *can't wait to catch up?* Or should I have added *P.S. Patrick was murdered about a month ago?*

I wanted to cancel, but I didn't, maybe because Nina had also invited her coworker as well as another friend I didn't know but apparently lived in the Chicago area. This would make it easier to act like everything was fine, so because of that, and the onset of cabin fever, I went.

In the beginning, I was enjoying myself. It felt nice to look my best for the first time in a while, and it was refreshing to be around people who didn't know what had happened. There weren't looks of pity; they weren't telling me how strong I was or that God had a plan for me. I was okay with God, but the only plan I'd ever counted on had evaporated, so the idea of a plan, even if it was the Lord Almighty's, didn't really appeal to me at the time.

We were just women enjoying the things we should be enjoying, and for a while, that was a fun distraction. But after dinner, we went to the bar next door and some sleazeball, probably twenty-five years our senior, stopped by the table to chat.

"We're all married," Nina informed him, politely but in a tone inviting him to get lost. My skin was crawling, and it had nothing to do with the man's sly grin. I became restless and suddenly uncomfortable in good company, probably because I felt like a liar, and the way I remedied that was to drink—and then drink some more. I hadn't been drunk in ages, and it wasn't something that had ever happened often, but by the time Nina's friend, Melody, commented that it was a good thing I'd come in a cab, I was buzzed enough to almost tell her how pretentious I thought it was that she named her son Einstein.

"Bet he never exceeds a *C* average," I whispered in Nina's ear, and her work friend, Lisa, must have overheard my comment and really enjoyed it, because with an entertained little grin on her face, she asked Melody how old she thought Einstein would be when he learned to spell his name.

"Oh, I don't know," Melody answered casually. But when she countered with, "I just wonder if you ladies will have learned to handle your alcohol by then," I realized there was a possibility I had more than whispered.

"Come on, Mel, don't be like that. We're just having fun." It seemed, according to more than a slight slur of speech, that Nina had resolved to make my number of drinks her number of drinks, and I think the main motivator was probably a marital rough patch she'd only hinted at earlier in the evening. Apparently Kevin was out of work and pressuring her for children, but anything more was left unsaid.

"Fun? You think insulting me is fun?"

"Get off your high horse. It's a joke," Nina replied, trying to end it, but then Lisa, naturally outspoken and now tipsy, asked Melody what she would name her high horse, and the three of us enjoyed a good cackle over it.

Now fuming, Melody glared at Nina as if she were the sole party responsible for everything that had been said. "You always were immature. I guess not much has changed, huh Nina?"

I wanted to pipe up, tell her she couldn't be more wrong. *Everything changes!* was at the tip of my tongue, but I sat there, mind swirling, buzz turning stale.

"You know, of all the things that could or should change, I thought your nose would be first on the list." *Nina! That was too far.* Lisa and I sat in entertained shock, but the insult war between the other pair waged on.

"You know, I should have your husband do it, and soon. I can't imagine there's a waiting list for a surgeon who lost his license on account of malpractice and sexual assault."

"Those charges are ludicrous and everyone knows it." I thought Nina might reach across the table and pummel Melody to the floor, but she held back her fists as much as she had her personal life, apparently.

"Does *everyone* include the *seven* women who've come forward?"

"Do you believe everything you hear?"

"No, but you must. Are you really that blind or just that desperate?"

It should have been Nina to burst away from the table and retreat to the bathroom, but embarrassingly enough, I made the trip instead. Melody had a terrible nose and an uninteresting personality. Lisa had permanent cheese breath and, from what I could tell, hated her job. Nina was apparently married to a cheating, possibly sex-addicted man, and the cherry on top was that she had a disloyal, hypersensitive now ex-best friend. But I was the one who had a dead husband, and no amount of plastic surgery or apologies could change the fact that I was going home to nothing, and not even the thought of the happy memories I once made there would make me want to slap these women into my reality any less.

With eyes bubbling over, I darted into the restroom and prayed no one would follow.

EIGHT

Julia

A FEW MINUTES in the restroom turned out to be good for me, although who knows if I'd been clearheaded enough to accurately keep time. No one had bothered me, but Nina did text: *u ok?* In a bit of a haze, I looked into the mirror and surmised that my makeup had made it through the tears okay enough but not completely unscathed.

I shuffled past a few ladies waiting in line, pushed open the restroom door, and who did I see standing against the corridor wall but Mr. Adrian No Last Name, which seemed to sober me up pretty quickly. He was looking right at me, leaving no way of escape, not that I really wanted to, so I just started walking toward him. The way he was staring, the look he had, I swear I almost died. I felt naked. That's what it was. I'd finally put my finger on what he'd been doing to me every time he was near. I was being seen with such intent, and it was a dizzying discomfort.

When I'd almost reached the place he was standing, he dropped his heel off the wall and took two steps forward until we were mere inches from each other. There he was, standing right before me with a grin, and before I could come up with something clever or interesting, he spoke.

"Hey tequila cheeks."

"Hey."

"Night going well?"

"I thought you were out of town?"

"I was. Happy to see you got the note."

I didn't know where to go from there, so I looked around the corner to see if the girls were still at the table.

"In a rush to get back to your friends?"

"Did you, like...follow me here?"

"No."

"Swear?"

"On the Bible, so will you stop answering my questions with questions?"

"I wasn't...I'm not doing that." We stared at each other and, although he seemed to be enjoying himself, I was getting dizzier by the second.

"Exactly how much did you drink tonight?"

"Not a lot."

"And you're getting home how?"

"Cab, don't worry."

"I'm not worried, and you're not going home in a cab."

"Oh, I'm not?"

"No, I'm taking you."

"You've got to be kidding, dude. I'm not letting you take me home."

"First of all...dude? And more importantly, you'd rather ride home alone with a Scandinavian or Moroccan or God knows what other kind of stranger than let me drive you?"

"That's racist."

"It's honest, and you know what I mean."

"Doesn't matter, you're trying to use the oldest trick in the book. *And*...I'm married." For the first time that night, I believed it.

"Just let me drive you home. I won't ask to come in. I'll drop you off and make sure you get inside safely," he promised, and I must have trusted him, because instead of fixating on all the reasons I shouldn't let him drive me home, I simply looked at him and gave a single, tipsy nod.

"I'll be out front in five minutes," I said.

Adrian

I honestly had no idea Julia would be at the bar that night. I'd just gotten back into town a few hours prior, stopped home for a shower, and made a stop at Bar 51 to talk business with one of my guys. We were in the back, and I just happened to look through the window of the kitchen door right in time to see Julia darting to the ladies' room.

By the time I got out there, which was almost instantly, Julia was out of sight and my mind spun with reasons she could've looked so upset. The thought that she might be on a date seemed impossible, but it was my first thought, and while scanning the crowd, I imagined beating some scumbag's head into tomorrow.

But no one seemed to fit the description, so I settled on a hunch Julia belonged to the three women—who, by the way, didn't look like fellow teachers—bickering at a high-top table.

I couldn't believe my luck or that she hadn't put up more of a fight, but there we were. I pulled to the curb and opened the passenger door; she put her hand on my forearm to steady herself as she got in the car, and even though I knew she wouldn't have done that in a more sober situation, it felt good.

She was being silly on the drive, and for once in our short history, Julia did all the talking and I just sat there, drinking it in. When we got to her place, I helped her unbuckle the seatbelt but left mine on.

"You're not going to walk me in?"

"I promised I'd stay in the car."

"Promises, promises," she said, her head becoming more and more difficult to hold up on her own.

"You'd never trust me again."

"I don't trust anybody. Everything is a lie." It came out effortlessly, and it seemed some kind of relief to her to have said it, a confession perhaps.

"Well that's...let's table that discussion," I suggested, reaching across to pop open the door.

"Just help me with the stairs," she said, looking longingly at the narrow, dimly lit steps at the front of her brownstone home.

I did as she requested, and when we got to the door, she unlocked it and turned to face me. Her eyes were getting droopier, and I knew she was minutes from sleep.

"I'm not really married," she admitted.

"You're not...?" I played along.

Julia closed her eyes and slowly shook her head back and forth, back and forth. "He's dead," she said and began nodding her head instead of shaking, but then she stopped. "Can you believe my husband got shot?"

Shot? Jesus. I didn't know. Why wouldn't Goldie tell me that part? "I *can't* believe that, Julia...I'm so sorry. I had no idea."

She opened her eyes only for tears to trickle out, and there was nothing that felt more natural than to take her in my arms, so I did. For a moment, I held her head to my chest, but eventually she pulled away and drunkenly told me that it was okay for me to like her, but it wasn't okay for her to like me. "I'm not on the market. It's only been a month. How long is a month? Is a month a long time? It feels like a long time...," she rambled.

I opened the door and motioned her inside. "Go to bed, sweet Julia," I said and kissed her on the cheek. She grinned and went inside, shutting the door behind her. "Two Tylenol and a glass of water first!"

Opening the door again for only a second, she popped her head out. "Goodnight."

Julia

Per Adrian's reminder, I took the Tylenol, but it didn't do much good, and I spent my entire Sunday switching between my bed and the couch, cursing myself the whole way. I was too old to be drinking like that, and what was it even worth? The night as a whole was okay; it started out fun, took some negative turns, and ended with a kiss on the cheek that, in the moment, sent chills throughout but, upon later, more sober reflection, had me gripped with guilt and frustration.

That was the most drunk I'd been since college, and even then drinking heavily was a rare occasion; it's just that I could bounce back much more quickly in those days. But now I felt like death, not to mention overwhelmed with regret. Remembering what I could of my conversation with Adrian made me cringe. I wondered if it was a mistake to tell him about Patrick's death and hoped it didn't send the wrong message. He seemed like a guy who'd take a mile if you gave him an inch, and I didn't want to be giving him anything.

Nina emailed that afternoon:

Hope you're feeling okay today...I'm a little under the weather. Was good catching up after a few years of not seeing you. I'm sorry about what happened with Melody. She can be such a killjoy sometimes, so don't feel bad about anything. Didn't realize someone was giving you a ride home—thought you were taking a cab, but I saw you getting into that guy's car. Does Patrick know him? If there's something going on, don't worry, I won't tell anyone, and truthfully, it might explain last night—it's unlike you to drink that much or talk about Patrick so little. I guess what I'm trying to say is, if you ever need to talk...give me a ring. Thanks to Melody, we all know I can probably relate to your situation somehow. Hope Patrick has a safe trip back from the conference. Tell him hello for me.

I couldn't breathe until I'd read the last word and, as soon as I did, quickly signed out of my account and tossed the laptop to the other end of the couch. Nina's inferences, however, bothered me for the rest of the day. I couldn't even be mad; I had lied. It's just that I never dreamed I'd end up getting in a car with Adrian and causing people to think I was having an affair—on my dead husband, no less! But she didn't know that, and I didn't know how to respond to her message, so I didn't.

Adrian met me at the diner the next four weeks straight, and not once did he ever make a move on me. He stayed in his booth and I in mine. Neither of us mentioned Patrick, and it was almost as if Adrian had kind of backed off a little. He was still showing up and would flirt every once in a while, but it was like now that he knew my circumstances, he considered himself—I don't know—watchman over them or something. Weird, but endearing.

Two weeks after Nina's first message, she emailed again: *Hope I didn't upset you. Just trying to help.*

I told Adrian about it, and he laughed. "Did you tell her to piss off?"

"I didn't say anything at all."

"Why?"

"I don't know, I...I don't want to tell her."

"Sounds like her schmuck of a husband is going to prison. I don't think you having an affair would ruffle her feathers, Julia."

"I'm *not* having an affair!" I was annoyed, and he seemed to get a kick out of it.

"What are you doing this weekend?" he asked.

"Not much. Relaxing."

"Not me."

"What does that mean?"

"It's just going to be a busy few days, that's all."

"Okay..."

"But I was thinking about something."

"Yeah?"

"Doesn't it seem like a waste that people think we're having a fling but all we ever do is sit here and eat at separate tables?"

Although I dreaded where the conversation was going, my lips curled into a grin. "It's not so bad."

"See, I knew you were enjoying yourself. You're mean

sometimes, you know."

"Mean?"

"Yes, mean. I'm talking about at first. But anyway, we're getting off track. What I'm saying is that we should go somewhere other than here."

"Like...where? To do what? I'm not going on a date with you."

"See, there's the meanness I was talking about."

"It's not mean. It's straightforward."

"Okay, I can respect that. But seriously, what do you like to do?"

NINE

Adrian

I'D TALKED JULIA into spending time with me outside the diner, but much to my dismay, she set that time for the crack of dawn the following Monday morning. When I showed up at her place, she was already waiting for me on the front steps.

"You're late."

"Give me a break, it's five after five."

"Like I said, late." She smirked, grabbing one elbow above her head to stretch. Julia was bright-eyed and bushy-tailed, but I hadn't yet been to bed, and even though that detail didn't exactly pair well with the fact that I hadn't done a cardiovascular workout in many, many moons, I was determined to put up a good showing. But by five minutes into our "jog," as Julia had named it,

I was running on complete empty. The girl was in shape, talking effortlessly, basically just plain smoking me. It was embarrassing, but I finally gave in and allowed myself to huff and puff as I needed.

Julia found it rather humorous. "Are you kidding me?"

"No, I'm not kidding you. Who do you think I am...?" I huffed, breathing louder than I care to admit. "Prefontaine?"

"You're the most out-of-shape person I know," she said, slowing down to walk with me.

"Possibly true but cold-blooded."

"The truth hurts, right?"

"I need coffee."

"Okay, there's a place around the corner," she said. "They're open early."

"No, no. I know a place. It's farther away but better."

"What's so great about it?"

"It's just better." We walked to the joint I was thinking of and placed our order. The barista, Jilly, knew to hand them over for free, an observation not lost on Julia, who gave me a suspicious look when I tossed a Benjamin in the tip jar, and it made me a little curious about when she'd put all the pieces together. She was smart, so it wouldn't be long. We drank our coffee and walked back to Julia's in silence.

I'm a person who usually acquires what he wants quickly, which of course had been my original plan with Julia. But a switch flipped when I learned that her husband had been murdered. I still wanted her, that was never a question, but I changed the game plan by putting it in her hands—not something I usually do, but I know what it's like to lose people, and not just lose them but have them taken from you. There's a difference.

So when we reached her place, instead of trying to kiss her

or ask her out or con my way inside, I simply clinked my coffee cup against hers, gave her a squeeze of the hand, and said, "See ya Friday."

"If you're not too sore to walk."

I drove home, enjoyed a glass of whiskey, and went to bed alone.

Julia

"All I'm saying is that I think you're moving too fast," Jennifer warned.

"It's nothing. We're friends."

"Friends don't take their friends out for a nothing dinner at Goodwin's, Julia. The salads alone are forty dollars."

"They are?" I pretended to be shocked. Another month had passed since Adrian went running with me, and since then we'd continued our weekly lunch. We hadn't been on any dates, but when he asked to hang out, I'd let him tag along to the grocery store or something similarly trivial and public (although I was constantly worried we'd be spotted together). Goldie was warming up to the idea of us getting to know one another, and I think she may have even been entertained by it, but still, her early warnings and the term *ladies' man* stuck with me.

Jennifer knew my loyalty toward Patrick, and she knew I was devastated. But what she didn't know was my loneliness. Our friends had been there for me, and they'd brought food and left messages, but week after week, the outreaching trickled away, and after a while, people just got back to their lives. It's natural, I get it, but I was completely alone in that house, and even when I was with friends, they treated me like, well, what I was: a widow—

everyone except Adrian, and I liked that.

I don't know exactly what it was that made me tell him I was ready to date, but I did. Three months wasn't enough time to be ready, and I wasn't, but I told him I was, I think because I was just so tired of being Patrick's widow instead of his wife, and I didn't want to live like that anymore. So Adrian took me to Goodwin's, and it was one of the best nights of my entire life. We went to a piano bar after dinner; the dueling pianos were entertaining, but when Adrian, standing behind me, slipped his arms around the small of my back and clasped his hands just under my belly button, it felt like everyone had shown up to watch us.

I got home that night and sailed into the kitchen. With a side of orange juice, I typed Nina an overdue message:

> *Thanks for inviting me to come out with you while you were in town. It was good for me, and I was sorry to hear about you and Kevin. As for the man who drove me home...there's something going on, but it's not what you think. Patrick died three months ago. He was shot during a robbery. I should have told you sooner, but it's just that, for one night, I thought it would be nice to not think about it. You can probably understand. Give my best to Kevin. I hope things get better for you.*

Every day with Adrian was fun or exciting in some way, and it wasn't just because he was a great distraction. Our relationship was a whirlwind that took flight about as quickly as Patrick had been taken from me. I was so happy in this phase of our relationship, and I know he was too. Everything in my world seemed to have been given new life; in fact, teaching was more joyful than before, even if Jennifer constantly nagged about my mental and emotional health. She wanted me to see a counselor and thought that dating again so soon was a big red flag. Maybe it was. Looking back, maybe it should have been.

Regardless, Adrian and I spent more time together than apart, and eventually, being with him felt more like a new normal than a temporary fantasy. We went to the nicest restaurants in town and even hole-in-the-wall places late at night. If there was a concert I wanted to see, we were there. When we went to clubs or events, we were let right in, no waiting in line, and our seats were always the best. At first I didn't think much of it; it was impressive and it felt good. I was having the time of my life and, quite frankly, falling in love.

That's why it didn't matter when he sat me down for a discussion about what he did for a living.

"I want to be upfront with you," he said.

"Okay," I encouraged, unaware of my naivety.

"I don't want you to look at me differently, but I want you to know the truth."

"The truth..."

"Yes."

"About what?"

"My business."

"Which is what?"

"It's a strip club, Julia."

"Oh," I said, taken back but not as much as he or I might have predicted. "Well...I don't really know what to say."

"Say anything you want."

"I don't want to say anything."

"Why? Don't be scared of hurting my feelings."

"I'm not, I just...which one?"

"Fancy's."

"Well at least it's one of the classier ones, from what I hear."

He laughed and seemed to relax. "Really? That's all you have to say?"

"What do you want me to say?"

"That you're not going to break up with me."

"I'm not going to break up with you." And I didn't. I didn't want to. The thought didn't even cross my mind until he said it. I wasn't crazy about the strip club, but at least it wasn't a whorehouse.

So we continued dating and things got serious fast. I think that's natural when you're older, when each person has a deep understanding of who they are. And when there's real chemistry, you don't need each other's statistics to come in and create something where there might not really be anything. I didn't care what he did for a living. Had he been a banker or a farmer or an astronaut, I wouldn't have been any more or less happy with him. I didn't need to analyze how we looked. All I knew was what I felt, and it felt really, really good.

TEN

Julia

ADRIAN AND I had been a couple for about six weeks when I got the call. My father's health had taken a turn and there wasn't much time. I needed to go home and face reality and, unfortunately, my mother. She would never understand or approve of my new relationship, and on most days I didn't either. It would have been nice to have Adrian there for moral support, but I wholeheartedly declined his offer to come along.

"Absolutely not," I said.

"Why not?"

"You know why not."

"Your mother?"

"That...and it would just be inappropriate."

"Screw inappropriate."

"Adrian...," I sighed, knowing my father was dying and my mother would be in rare form. There was no need to tip either one over the edge.

"I know," he said. "Do what needs done."

I flew to Connecticut and it was nothing but terrible. "You look terrible," was actually the first thing my mother said to me when I stepped through the door. Was it because she suspected I'd spent the past three months not eating, not sleeping—but yes, drinking my widowed life away—or was she just being her usual self? I went straight to my father's bedside, and as I sat there, my hands outstretched to hold one of his, I couldn't help but think, *he looks terrible.*

Our neighbor, Mrs. Shirley, who'd lived next door since before I was even born, had called me the week after Patrick died. "I'm so sorry, sweetheart." Some people have a way of warming you, and Mrs. Shirley's scratchy voice did just that. "Know that I'm thinking of you, dear," she said, and I knew she meant it, because I was probably twelve or thirteen when her own husband passed and she'd been living alone since.

I thanked her and asked about my parents.

"Oh, honey, they're fine...doing just fine."

"Are you sure?"

"They'd probably love to see you, but...you know, they're fine."

A twinge of guilt raced through me, because I knew I hadn't visited as often as I should have or even as often as I wanted. And when I did visit, it was really only because I missed my dad. I wanted to see Mom too, held out hope that the next time would be different, but it never was, so I avoided her as much as possible.

"I plan to visit soon...I'm sure I won't have trouble getting time off work," I admitted to Mrs. Shirley.

"Oh, that would be nice. We'd all love to see you again. But Julia, just take care of yourself, sweetie...you've got some...you know, mending to do."

I was tearing up a bit because of her kindness and because of the guilt but also because I was afraid to know the answer to what I asked next.

"How does he look?"

"Well...he has good days."

"I mean...Mrs. Shirley, does he still look like my dad?" I gripped the phone, wondering what the time since I'd last been home had done to him.

She paused but gave it to me straight. "He doesn't look well, sweetie."

"How long do you think it will be?" I asked, my voice timid.

"From what I hear, probably not long. But you never can tell with these types of things. It could be a month; it could be a year."

I couldn't speak, and I didn't know how to admit what Mrs. Shirley must have known I was thinking.

"It's okay if you don't come back, Julia. It's a nice gesture, and when it's all said and done, maybe you'll have less regret, but...you know, sometimes it's better to remember our loved ones the way they were. Seeing them like that...well honey, you don't forget it."

She was right. My father was dying right in front of me now, and although I was glad to have that last week with him, there was a part of me that desperately wished to unsee it.

My mother obsessed over every detail of the calling hours and funeral, worrying herself to no end over whether or not there would be a good turnout. She hoped—to my surprise, out loud—that she would say the right thing and remember everyone's name. And then there was the sock debate, over which she spent an hour digging through my father's immaculately organized drawer, and another forty-five minutes deciding between black and blue, all without shedding a single tear.

The night after the funeral, we sat in the kitchen drinking hot tea, and she finally cracked. Thankfully, I was there to witness the living proof that she was in fact human, but unfortunately, Helen High-on-Emotion found an outlet and punching bag in me.

"You know Julia," she sobbed, "your father was sick and you hardly ever came home. What kind of daughter does that make you?"

"I was just here four months ago."

"Yes, months! *Months*, Julia! You ought to be ashamed of yourself."

"Mom...I called...I talked to Dad a lot...he said not to come...I did what I could. I..."

"Don't stutter like an uneducated person, Julia. I raised you better than that."

"Mother, don't."

"Don't what? Don't say the truth, because it might hurt your feelings? Don't you think it hurt your father's feelings that his one and only child hardly ever came to see him?" She leaned in, her face now so close to mine. "He was dying anyway, but you know what, he probably died sooner than he had to because of you," she jeered.

"Don't be like this tonight," I said, tears trickling down my cheeks.

"I have a right to be however I want, thank you. My husband is *dead!*"

She threw the napkin holder across the room, but before the two-ply, fanned paper had a chance to settle on the floor, I stood and marched to the side kitchen door. "That makes two of us," I said and walked out.

The only thing I'd ever truly loved about home was dead and gone, and because of that I was thankful my return flight was booked to leave exactly twelve hours after Helen's tantrum.

I'd left her in the kitchen and gone outside to get fresh air, but nothing about her stupid backyard bench surrounded by flowers she probably kissed before bed each night seemed revitalizing in the least. Sighing, I looked up to the darkened spring sky and wondered if I could ever come back to this place. Just then, Mrs. Shirley's corner light came on, and she stepped out onto the screened back porch.

"Would you like some tea, sweet girl?"

"Already had some. Didn't settle." I stood from the bench with a half grin and made my way over to her yard.

She opened the screen door. "How 'bout some vodka?"

"Seriously?" I laughed.

"Seriously, now sit your buns down and wait just one minute," she instructed, smacking one of the patio chair cushions as if to unsettle the dust. I did as she said and giggled to myself as she stepped back into the house, wearing quilted slippers, a floral nightgown under a terrycloth bathrobe, and approximately seven hair curlers, of which only some seemed rightfully placed. She returned a moment later with pre-poured glasses and sat in the chair next to mine.

"There we go. Two fingers for me, three for you," she said.

"Three for me...you must have heard my mother and me."

"A little," she admitted. "Only caught bits and pieces, but it's hard to tell what came out of that mouth."

"She says Dad probably died sooner than he had to because of me. I broke his heart, I guess."

"Hold on, I'll be right back," she said, holding a finger in the air, only to return with the bottle she'd just poured from. "Just in case."

"Mrs. Shirley!" I laughed.

"A little extra hooch never hurt in times like these."

"I'm sure it has."

"Well, that's probably right, but you're not a drunk or a druggie, are you?"

"No."

"Well then, you'll be fine."

We both took a sip, and I went on feeling miserable about my lot as Helen's daughter. "How have you lived next door to her this whole time and managed to still be her friend?"

"Oh, honey, I wouldn't say we're friends."

"But you're neighborly...and didn't you used to go to gardening shows together?"

"We did. But that was years ago, and besides...if you have to be neighbors, might as well be nice, right?"

"I suppose."

"I always sort of got a kick out of trying to figure her out. It was like a psychology experiment."

"And what did you discover?"

"That it will take someone with more training...perhaps a whole team of scientists."

"Amen to that." I raised my glass.

"But, you know, the years have a way of showing you who a

person really is...and next-door neighbors hear things. I know your mother is a...well, Helen is just Helen, a most complicated woman. I used to get so upset when you were a girl, the way she'd yell at you."

"You heard her?"

"Oh yes, I heard her, loud and clear. And then she'd come waltzing out the next morning and we'd talk about roses and silly things like that, and all the while, I wanted to wring her neck, but I just kept on pretending I thought she was the queen she thinks she is."

I laughed out loud and asked, "Why do you think you kept up the act?"

"Oh, I don't know. Some people just aren't worth the effort. Can't fix 'em, can't change 'em, they're going to do what they want. And plus...a person has to be downright filled with suffering to make other people that miserable, don't you think?"

"I think you have a point there, Mrs. Shirley."

"I always wondered...what were her parents like?"

"Her father was okay, I guess, but the way I hear it, her mother was wretched."

"Not surprising, but it explains a lot."

"She hardly ever talks about it. And another thing...I bet she never told you that my dad was married once before her."

"Must have slipped her mind."

"Yup. My uncle, well, he's dead now, but he told me that Mom had a crush on Dad all through high school, but he married another girl from their town. Two years into it, she went off the rails and split. He seemed to think it was spurred on by a miscarriage. Anyway, Daddy eventually married again and Mom made him move to Connecticut because she couldn't stand the way people looked at her."

"Well now, that explains even more."

"Aren't you glad you got me drinking?"

"Yes. Oh yes."

"Mom was thirty-five when she had me."

"No spring chicken by the standards of those days."

"Right, and she reminds me of it every chance she gets. They had agreed to not have children but then Daddy insisted."

"Well, he was a good man. Loved the snot outta you, really he did. But now he's dead and there's nothing we can do about it, so let's talk about something else."

Maybe some would be offended by what seemed a flippant remark, but Mrs. Shirley knew I could benefit from a change of subject. "Okay. What should we talk about?"

"Your love life." No hesitation there.

"My love life?" I asked, pretending to be shocked and slightly displeased.

"Yes, are you seeing anyone?"

"It really hasn't been long enough."

"But there is someone, yes?" Just then I remembered slipping out back to take a call from Adrian. We'd stayed on the line for maybe a half hour, and even though I was downtrodden, we missed each other and the conversation had turned mushy-gushy.

"You heard me on the phone the other night, didn't you?"

"I'm telling you, next-door neighbors hear things, chickadee. So who is he?"

Unbothered by the eavesdropping, I went on to share a few basic details.

"Well he sounds nice. Is he a looker?"

"He's nice looking, yes." I smiled. "But...he's not like Patrick. Not at all."

"What does that matter?"

"I don't know, I guess it doesn't."

"Let me tell you, it doesn't," she said, seeming rather passionate. "Sometimes the best thing you can do is go with the unexpected choice."

"I don't think Mr. Shirley was exactly unexpected."

"Oh no, honey he was as square as they come. I loved him with all my heart, but the man was a bore."

"Mrs. Shirley!"

"Oh, come on, he knew it, and it's not like I'm talking behind his back, God rest his soul, because he told me so the day he proposed marriage. Made this gallant-sounding speech: 'Well Noreen, I know I'm not as big of an adventure as Ted, but I do love you, and I want to take care of you and Josie. I want you to be my wife.' It was so cute how he had to really rev himself up to even say it."

"Wait, what? Who's Ted? Josie was already born?"

"Oh, you thought Josie was a Shirley? Well, she is but not by blood. Ted is her biological father and my first love. Except he almost wasn't, because I damn near married someone else."

"What?" The surprises just kept coming.

"It's a bit of a story," she said, taking a gulp from her glass. "Well, it was 1953, and I was twenty years old, working as a legal secretary. My boss was trying to free this bank robber from prison, and he did just that. So the bank robber is roaming free and of course getting into more legal trouble here and there, and because my boss was so good at his job the first go 'round, Ted came back to him again and again."

"The bank robber was Ted?!"

"Yup, I fell for the crook all right. He was handsome and wicked clever and made me laugh all the way out of my chair. I'd been dating another fella, Eli, who was a pretty fair catch, and things between us had gotten sort of serious about the time Ted came along. Everyone thought I was going to marry Eli, and truth be told, so did I. But when he asked, I told him I'd have to think about it."

"Bet that went over well."

"Oh yeah, he really loved it." She winked. "But he was patient and understood I wasn't ready, and I carried on dating two men at once, each one more different than the other. But then one day, Eli caught me out to dinner with Ted and told me I had to make a choice right then and there. Well, of course I chose Ted, and I felt bad for hurting Eli...but that's how it all shook out."

"So what happened with Ted?"

"We were together another year or so, and it was the wildest, most exciting time of my life. Everyone thought I was crazy for passing on Eli, and my parents told me I was playing with fire. They never did like Ted, and for good reason. I got pregnant, and although he said he'd marry me, he eventually took off. I understood. It was hard, but your mother is your mother and Ted was Ted, so I knew why it never could be with him. A few months after Josie was born, I met Mr. Shirley, and less than a year later, we were married."

"And what happened to Ted?"

"Well, funny thing, he started robbing banks again. Mr. Shirley and I returned from our honeymoon and bought a house. I was cooking dinner that first night in the new place, this place, and Mr. Shirley came walking in the house carrying the newspaper, which I didn't even notice until he plopped it on the counter. Put it right next to the sink and walked away. There I was peeling potatoes, looked over, and right on the front page, in letters that couldn't get any bigger: 'BANK ROBBER SHOT DEAD MID-HEIST.' We got in bed that night and Mr. Shirley asked if I was happy in the new house. I told him I was but that it came as no surprise because I was good at picking. We got naked and never talked about Ted again until it was time to tell Josie, but that was all."

"Wow. That's..."

"Surprising?"

"Yes."

"Because I play the organ at church, is that why?"

"Well...yeah, pretty much."

"Oh, sometimes I forget all about it."

"And you don't regret any of it?"

"Oh, honey, no. Ted broke my heart, but it was a thrill and, had I been a little wiser, I wouldn't have gotten Josie. Mr. Shirley kept all his promises, and we took care of each other. That, my girl, is its own adventure."

On the verge of tears sweeter than I'd cried all day, I smiled. "And Eli?"

"What about him? He turned out to be a stupid ole prick."

ELEVEN

Julia

I'D ALWAYS BEEN a nervous passenger, but for once I walked on the plane not thinking of the probability of crashing or the prospect that the pilot had had one too many drinks the night before or that a mechanic had, I don't know, sneezed or something, lost his place on the preflight checklist, and forgotten to inspect a crucial part of the plane that would ultimately lead to an engine fire and all of our deaths. It was freeing, and yet the flight couldn't end soon enough.

Falling in love again was exciting but came with its own share of guilt. I was anxious to return to Chicago, and it should have been because I wanted to be back in the sanctuary that was the home I'd shared with Patrick. But no, I was simply excited to see

Adrian. It was too soon to be in love with someone else, or at least that's what my conscience continually reminded me. I should still have been grieving the loss of my husband, and now my father, and to an extent, I was. But grief is tiring, and Adrian was life. He made me forget. He made me happy.

He picked me up at the airport and took me home to shower before dinner. He'd offered takeout, thinking I might be too tired to be out and about, but I said a nice dinner would do me good, and it did. It was a lovely evening—until it wasn't.

The valet had brought the car around to the front of the restaurant, and Adrian was helping me in when his phone rang. He looked at the screen and answered it, and just before he shut my door, I heard him say, "Hey Dom, what's up?" It was a casual call, or so I thought, until Adrian darted around to the driver's side, got in, slammed the door, and sped down the street without saying a word.

"Adrian?" I asked, worried. "What's happening? What's wrong?" I was scared because he looked scared, and Adrian was never scared.

"Julia," he started, steadying his voice. "I'm going to need you to do me a favor, okay?"

"Okay, yes, anything."

"One of my guys is hurt. We're gonna pick him up, and we're gonna get him some help, and I need you to stay calm, okay?"

"Okay," I gulped, somehow knowing not to ask further questions, not that I really could, since I was holding my breath as Adrian blew through stoplights.

We arrived at an abandoned warehouse I didn't recognize, and Adrian instructed me to stay in the car. He jogged around for a moment, disappeared, and then came out of the building lugging a man strewn over his shoulder. I got out and opened the back door so Adrian could toss the guy in, and it was then that I saw the bullet wounds in his abdomen.

The tires squealed and churned against the gravel, and we fishtailed, causing the backseat mystery man's groans to turn into screams.

"Hold on, Two Guns, we're gonna get you a doctor."

Two Guns? I shot Adrian a look.

"I'm sorry, Adrian. I called Dominic. I didn't want to bother you."

"It's okay, buddy, I was closer. Dom wouldn't have made it in time."

"Yeah, well, verdict's still out on you, ain't it?" The guy huffed, struggling to breathe.

"Don't you worry about that. We're getting there."

I looked at Adrian, then to the back seat, and back at Adrian. *This is crazy.*

"So what happened back there?" Adrian asked.

"Adrian, they set us up. There were supposed to be two guys..."

"Yeah, I know."

"But there were four...we gave 'em the stuff, but they didn't want to pay...so things got physical..."

"I can see that."

"And Johnny...he'd have been fine but...got a little overzealous, put his gun in one of their faces...it didn't end well."

"So they shot you too, for good measure?" I asked, and I swear Adrian grinned.

"Yup...but I got one of 'em, I think...I..." Two Guns trailed off and passed out, and without even thinking, I unbuckled my seatbelt and climbed into the back.

"Just keep him awake, Julia. Only a few more minutes."

I smacked his cheeks and kept him alert until the car stopped, and when I looked up, I was surprised to see that we weren't at a hospital. A man came out of a late seventies-style mansion and helped Adrian bring Two Guns inside. The dining room table was already set up with blankets and medical instruments, and I assumed it was Dominic who had given the heads up. Dr. Arredondo went to work right away, and it wasn't until Dominic showed up and had a private word with Adrian off in the corner that I looked down and noticed the blood on my hands and dress.

We left shortly after, but Dom stood watch through the night. Back at my place, I asked for an explanation but knew I may be better off not knowing.

"Okay, so what's going on?"

"With what specifically."

"Let's start with this Two Guns guy."

"Pretty good nickname if you ask me. Tony Two Guns just rolls off the tongue, don't you think?"

"Yeah, it's a real charmer."

"But of course, somewhere along the way it was shortened to simply Two Guns, which is still an awesome name. Anyway, he got it in a pretty straightforward way...one day he woke up to two guys standing at the end of his bed, one on the left, one on the right. Each guy had a gun pointed in his face, and they said they'd give him a head start. He was allowed to make one move and then they'd shoot him. Well...I'm sure they knew there was a gun under the covers, but sure to God they didn't figure he had two. Tony reached for both, one on each side, and before those idiots could finish a cackle, he pulled the triggers and sent duck feathers flying. Dropped 'em both. Single-kill shot, each one. Dammit, I love that story. Gives me chills."

"Adrian..."

"Come on, it's a great story!"

"I agree, and maybe in the morning I'll find it more entertaining, but look at me," I said, holding up my bloodstained hands.

"Okay...I get it...you're disturbed. That's normal. Maybe you should just...shower and go to bed. We can talk about this tomorrow."

He kissed me, and for whatever reason, I did what he said. He called the next morning and asked if I was doing all right. I said I was, which was only half a lie, and then he told me he'd forgotten to tell a detail of Two Guns' story, that the guys who showed up to Tony's house were simply there to collect a gambling debt. "Everyone's got a weak spot...and for him, it's those damn horses. Always has been," he said, brushing it off.

"He doing okay?"

"Dom says he'll be good as new in a few months."

We started talking about something else—what, I can't remember, but I knew right away we wouldn't soon discuss what happened with Two Guns or Dr. Arredondo. It reminded me of a story Nina told the night she was in town. Apparently she'd come home eleventh-grade drunk and her mother told her to go to bed, that they'd talk about it in the morning. "Well," Nina laughed. "It's been seventeen years and we still haven't talked about it!"

Adrian was running so much more than a strip club, I knew that now. He was more than what I had thought, and I should have put it together sooner. But who, in a logical line of reasoning, would make such a leap? There were negative consequences, sure, and a list of serious repercussions on the line, but I was already too in love for them to matter.

I didn't care about the consequences, and it didn't feel wrong. It felt like he'd warmed me, like I'd been running on a damp, rainy day, and suddenly, because of a steamy tub of water, my frigid skin had softened on account of full immersion, and I considered myself baptized. The old me was gone, and it seemed I'd never relapse. But like all sinners, I was wrong.

PART TWO

TWELVE

Julia

DATING A NEW person means the inevitable process of meeting their friends. Sometimes these friends tell you quite a bit about your new flame, and with Adrian this was the case. It's not so much what these friends actually say; it's learning about who they are that really clues you in, and these friends in particular were a close-knit group—no outsiders allowed.

By the time I got to know Adrian's crew, I had already figured out what they were all about, but their wives and girlfriends confirmed it. Leave it to a woman to say the thing an entire group of men won't say aloud. The men would say, "Our thing," or, "He's a friend of ours," but most of their wives, after nothing more than a single vodka tonic, would tell you their lives were eyebrow deep in the mob. This was all behind closed doors, of course. Don't get me wrong, these ladies were as stealthy and quick as the men they lived for, and they knew the street as well as anyone. An hour with these women was an education, and they taught me everything Adrian couldn't.

Adrian couldn't relay the sentiment behind what it's like to watch your husband go away to prison. To the people in this lifestyle, the men especially, incarceration wasn't met with the same taboo as it was to the outside world. For the men, it was a badge of honor, an earning of stripes, if you will, and most of the women came to accept it as an occupational hazard. But still, despite the fact that the family still took care of them, it was the women who suffered the most. Many grew up interacting with their fathers in the confines of a visitation room, and now they explained to their own children why Daddy couldn't be at home for a while.

It was sad and then, at times, bizarre, like the day my new friend, Ariana, showed up at the school parking lot with her seven-month-old, Lucas, in tow to ask if I'd watch him for the night. Apparently one of her breast implants was leaking, and she found a surgeon who would fix it at a discount and with no money down. The payment plan wouldn't begin for another ninety days, and by then her husband would be out of jail and able to pay it off. She was telling me all this and my mind was spinning, trying to come up with the words to suggest maybe she shouldn't go to the discount doctor, but Lucas's bags were already packed, and Ariana had them loaded in my car before I could say a thing.

I returned Lucas to her house the next day only to find that the surgeon had not only attempted to fix the leaky implant but had also performed liposuction and a tummy tuck and injected lip fillers. I couldn't even look at her, almost vomited when she mumbled, "Sorry Julia, the other sitter cancelled...could you watch Lucas for a few more days?" I thought those ballooned lips would just explode any second. She couldn't even close her mouth. Lucas started crying and I had to get out of there, so I told her to call me later. I called a mutual friend, Liz, and she spent the next several days with Ariana, who soon found herself in the emergency room. It turned out that the discount surgeon was neither certified nor insured and, I could only guess, had never even won a round of the childhood board game Operation.

Needless to say, he didn't get paid, but we found a better doctor, and I kept watching Lucas when I could. Within a few weeks, Ariana went from a mangled, swollen mummy back to her usual self: the life of the party, who now shared exact measurements with Barbie.

We spent a lot of time hanging out with the group, but Adrian still liked to plan extravagant dates for just the two of us. Everything he did was over the top, which was of course exciting at first, but eventually it was just exhausting. One day he asked what I'd like to do and I suggested we go to the ballpark. "Okay, great idea," he said. "I'll get tickets."

"No," I said emphatically, "*I'm* getting the tickets."

"Okay...," he smirked. "Why are *you* getting the tickets?"

"Because you'll probably rent a box or something, or bully someone out of their front row seats, and I just want to show up to the game, eat a hot dog, and sit in a regular seat, that's all. Nothing fancy, just...regular."

"We're not regular people, but that's fine. If that's what you want..."

That was what I wanted, and our simple evening at the ballpark was what I got. Thank God. Adrian made jokes about needing binoculars, but all in all, it was a fantastic evening. It felt normal, which is something I hadn't felt in a long time, and it was nice. It reminded me of my dad, because he played in college and used to coach my softball team, and it reminded me of Patrick, who'd always been a die-hard fan of baseball. Choosing the ballpark made me feel less guilty, like I was saying to Patrick, *I haven't forgotten you.* I spent hours and hours in a ballpark with him and my father, so spending that night at Wrigley Field with Adrian was like introducing everyone. The Cubs were my team, but the night was special to me for more than just that reason, and I think Adrian could sense it.

He was always buying me things whether I needed them or not, and there was no limit to the range of items he'd gifted me. I liked the new refrigerator, but where was I supposed to put a full-size massage chair? The girls were over one day when I happened to mention that it took up too much space and I hardly ever used it.

"Well, you better save it," one of them advised.

"Why?" I asked. "I don't really like it."

"If Adrian goes away or breaks your heart or something, you can hock it." *Duh*, she seemed to be saying, *get with the program.*

Okay, valid point, but which pawn shop specializes in likely stolen goods, and how the heck would I even get the chair there? Doesn't matter, the point was that this was the way these women thought, and I wondered if I should start thinking that way too. It seemed crazy, but at the end of the day, it wasn't. It was smart, and that's what made me feel insane.

My new friends seemed to be looking out for me and had an unexpected way of injecting confidence where I might have had doubts. They always had an answer for my many questions and, when the need arose, knew a guy who knew a guy. Even my relationship with Adrian was celebrated, which was something

I really appreciated, because with this group of women, it could have easily gone another way.

"Oh, Julia, you and Adrian are like peanut butter and jelly. You just go together," one friend said.

"No, no," another chimed in. "They're more like...the internet and cat videos. Unlikely pair, but it works." She giggled. "But anyway, have you seen the hits on those cat videos?"

Going to nice places and doing things the average person doesn't do was easy, while the war within and the chaos of organized crime was hard. Adrian came to my house one day and said I couldn't talk to a girl named Maura Costello anymore.

"Why?"

"Her husband's a goddamn snitch, that's why." That was that. The snitch was gone and Maura was shunned completely. "So if she calls...don't help her, Julia. She's dead to you."

Maura showed up at my house the very next day, and I pretended not to hear the doorbell or her run-down comments. "Come on Julia, I know you're in there," she said, but I literally sat on the floor behind my easy chair and cried, and apparently some of the other girls shared a similar experience. Disloyalty for the purpose of loyalty is a tough pill to swallow.

But we also had fun—so much that I'd all but forgotten about my old friends. I thought of them only occasionally and usually only to wonder what they'd think if they saw me now. In the beginning, I'd sometimes call them back, but I eventually stopped doing that and they stopped trying. It wasn't personal; it was a natural drift. Plus, I'd led them to believe I'd taken on all these extra roles at the school, but that was a lie. I felt bad about that, but I'd never done anything quite as luxurious or fun with them as what I was doing now. It was intoxicating. Adrian was intoxicating, and he made me feel, for the first time, intoxicating in my own right.

Nothing was the same as it was before. My husband had died and I had gone to sleep, but Adrian came along and woke me up. Deep down, I knew he was trouble. I knew he was nothing like Patrick had been, but they did share something in common, and that was loving me. And I loved him.

Being with Adrian was heavenly, and yet I knew he was far from sainthood. But then, so are all of us. Maybe that's what I told myself. Maybe I let my own simple sin be the reason to overlook Adrian's. "You worry too much," he often said to me and, with that one line, relayed this message: my sin is much worse than yours and it's not keeping me awake at night, so close your innocent little eyes and dream of sweeter things.

THIRTEEN

Adrian

IN THIS LIFE, you have to know yourself. You have to beat everyone to the punch, because it's not a matter of if your weaknesses will be used against you but a question of when. As a man with far fewer weaknesses than most, I used that to my advantage, but even I had soft spots, places to be poked, and every once in a while, someone took a jab.

My soft spot was that I didn't have a family. For some, this very fact made them the ultimate soldier, because they had nothing to lose, nothing hanging over their head, and maybe most importantly, no shaky needle struggling to point their conscience compass due north. But the fact that I was all alone wasn't a strength of mine, and the hardness I was mostly made up of wasn't the reason I didn't have a family. I didn't have a family because they were taken from me.

It was years ago, when I was somewhere between rookie and pro. I could hardly remember that version of myself. He was a good person, a go-getter. He'd done some bad things, sure, but his heart was still good and he believed in good things. I didn't know what kind of things I believed in now. I said that I did, but…all I knew now was Julia.

My family was taken from me and Julia's from her, so maybe that's why it was easier for me to tell her what happened, how I never saw it coming.

My dad was a well-respected capo, and he deserved every ounce of what he had. When he said jump, his men asked how high and how many times, and they didn't dare roll an eye. He was grooming me, sure, but he made me work for every little bit, was harder on me than he was everybody else, and there wasn't a thing I didn't love about that.

The streets had gotten out of hand. It's called organized crime, but these were times of shifting sand and turf wars. Tempers had never been shorter and the egos of grown men never more fragile. It's just something that happens every once in a while. Every day on the street is survival of the fittest, but this was an extreme event, like a dinosaur extinction type of time.

Christmas Eve came around, and there were hams that hadn't made it to their destinations, so my dad wanted me to deliver them myself. "Show your face," he'd said. "Let the people know we care about 'em." That was my dad to a tee. If the books were short, he'd kill you, but until then, he really did care.

Mrs. Spencer, a bakery owner, gave me a dozen donuts, and Bruce Littman gave me a six-pack of beer. Jenny Milhoan, widow to one ill-prepared man and mother to three hungry children, smiled at the ham and then gave a thankful set of tears when she felt the roll of hundred-dollar bills I'd slipped into our neighborly handshake.

I was feeling pretty cheery, and that was even before I stopped by the bar for a few quick shots with a buddy of mine. We, late as usual, got in the car and drove to my parents' house for their big Christmas party. We saw the smoke before we saw the house. I sped up, screeched onto the curb, and barely got the car in park.

Someone—and I knew immediately who it was—had smuggled a bomb into the party via a caterer. It detonated just minutes before my arrival. I should have been there, should've been dead, but instead, there I was, looking at charred bones and a flaming Christmas tree. People go to therapy to get over seeing shit like that—and I don't blame them. But what I had to do didn't cost me by the hour.

I retaliated, killed a lot of people, more than I ever had, all in freezing cold blood. I was a monster, and I did what I had to do. And then one day, Dom's pop called me up.

"You get 'em all, Adrian?"

"As many as I'm gonna."

"Good. Good for you."

"Yeah...good for me." It was a sad statement for a man so supposedly satisfied over the blood on his hands.

"Time for a change of scenery, don't you think?"

"Got something in mind?"

"Come on out here, will ya?"

"Last I heard, Chi-town was full. Running like a well-oiled machine, they say."

"Yeah, yeah, well-oiled my ass. Got a spot for you, Adrian."

"Appreciate the offer, but I'd really have to think about it."

"Think about it for how long?"

"New York is home."

"I get it...I really do. But you know...home is...well it ain't ever gonna be the same again, is it boy?"

I couldn't argue with that. My parents, my siblings—every living relative I'd had was at that party, not to mention most of my father's crew. It would take years to rebuild, and by then, what would really be left for us? The higher-ups were saddened by what had been lost, but there was nothing they could do. The bomb was retaliation for some things my father had done, and the crime family heads declared it a wash. Enough was finally enough; the war was over, so they said.

I got justice on my own, so what then? I didn't want to leave New York, but I wanted to leave. I held out a few months, and then I packed up and moved to Chicago, where I got a new family, a second chance, and in the long run, Julia. She wasn't just a soft spot; she was my Achilles' heel, the orchestrator of destruction I never saw coming.

FOURTEEN

Julia

I RAN INTO Patrick's old boss, Brandon Sloan, at the grocery store. He was preoccupied with the yogurt section, which tempted me to dart in another aisle and act as though I hadn't seen him, but he turned at the last second and our eyes met.

"Brandon, how are you?" I asked, faking delight. He was a nice enough guy and Patrick never had a problem with him, but running into people from our married life had a way of knocking the wind out of me.

"Hi, Julia. So good to see you. I'm doing okay, but more importantly, how are you?"

More importantly? Gag me with a spoon. "I'm well, thanks. How's Mandy?"

"Oh, doing great. A little cranky...she's pregnant."

"Congratulations, that's fantastic!"

"Thanks...thanks, we're really excited."

"I bet so..." I trailed off, unsure of what to say, and I knew by the look on his face that he didn't either. "And things at work are good?"

"Oh yeah...yeah, yeah, things are fine. We miss Patrick, that's for sure..."

I smiled, again unsure of what to say, and maybe on another day, what he'd said would've made me sad. Brandon seemed to focus now on the diamond studs I was wearing, and as his gaze slid down my arm and into the shopping cart where a brand new Louis Vuitton handbag gently sat, I knew he was thinking about the fact that I was a widowed school teacher employed by a private Christian academy, not to mention he knew, right down to the dime, Patrick's old salary.

"Life insurance came through, huh?"

"Umm...yes," I admitted. *Like it's any of your business.* "But these were a gift..." Awkwardness surged through me as I reached a hand gently to my ear.

"Oh, oh sure...yeah, I don't know why I...I'm sorry, that was rude."

"It's okay. Really it's fine," I said, gripping the shopping cart now, preparing to say a farewell.

"But everything finally came through all right with that, yes?"

"Oh yeah."

"Good, I was worried about it when they came to the office."

"Oh. Wait, Brandon, who came to the office?"

"The insurance company."

"When?"

"Few weeks ago...maybe three. Geez, when was it?" he asked himself, concentrating as if my main concern was the exact date, when really I was alarmed because the life insurance check had come through relatively quickly and without issue.

"What kinds of questions did they ask?"

"Oh...just...I don't know, weird stuff if you ask me, but then again I'm not in that business, so..."

"Weird stuff?"

"Yeah...like, was Patrick a good worker...what did I think of him...did I know of any affairs or marital problems...were there drug or gambling issues. Actually, they asked what I thought of you, too."

"Why would they ask that? That's strange," I said with a growing pit in my stomach.

"Probably just standard procedure considering the way...the way he died, you know. No stone unturned when it comes to unusual deaths, I would guess. We'd probably be surprised what some people would kill their spouses for, Julia."

"Yeah...yeah, I guess we would."

He changed the subject to Greek yogurt. "Is it just a fad, or do you think there's really something to it?"

I told him I thought it was supposed to be healthier, and then I excused myself and went on my way. It seemed plausible that the insurance company would do their due diligence ruling out fraud, but still, something didn't sit well with me. The timeline was off. I crossed the remaining items off my shopping list and wheeled into a checkout aisle, which, as luck would have it, was also Brandon's checkout aisle.

"Congratulations again about the baby," I said, smiling as I unloaded the cart.

"Thanks, Julia, I really appreciate that."

He slid his credit card through the machine, and as we all waited for the receipt to appear, I spoke up. "The people that came into the office...how many of them were there?"

"Oh, just one."

"Man or woman?"

Confused, he answered that it was a man.

"What did he look like?"

"Does it matter?" he asked, taking the receipt from the cashier.

"Maybe not. I'm just curious."

"Decent-sized guy...in a suit...sorry, I'm not good with details like that. But you know, now that I think about it...it wasn't your typical office guy."

"But he was in a suit?"

"Yeah, a nice one. And longish hair...kind of a dirty blond."

"Is that so?" I asked, feeling my jaw tighten up.

"Yeah. Stranger things have happened though, right?"

"Yeah...stranger things."

I went home and scrubbed the bathroom until my back ached and my fingers were raw and shriveled. Adrian was coming over for dinner; I hadn't decided what to do with my newfound knowledge but was leaning toward not saying anything right away.

An hour later, just as I was finishing the shrimp alfredo, Adrian walked in and I greeted him like normal. He went into the living room, slipped out of his suit jacket, and laid it carefully across the back of the couch. From the corner of my eye, I watched as he casually paced around the room, relaying to me the events of his day thus far, of course in limited detail.

"Did you know Caponella's wife has a third nipple?"

"How would I know that?" I asked, loud enough for only myself to hear.

"Well, she *used* to have a third nipple...got it removed."

"Lots of people are born with extra nipples," I said, louder this time. "Sometimes they just look like moles or something."

"Yeah well, apparently hers was a full-fledged nipple. You could probably get milk to come out of it."

"Poor Doris. That's terrible of you to say," I added, clearly annoyed with him.

"Yeah well, what's terrible is that she had to go back in because the scar got infected."

"How do you even know this? You men gossip more than any woman I've ever met."

"Whoa, whoa, whoa...Cap told me himself. Wanted me to know there was a legit reason he needed a day off."

I stirred fresh ground pepper into the pasta and tried to catch my breath, exhaling some of my frustration so that he wouldn't ask what was the matter.

"Anyway," he said, "how was your day?"

"Fine. Nothing too fancy."

"Hmmm...sounds boring."

I rolled my eyes and turned the stovetop to low heat.

"Anyway...not to be a jerk, Julia, really, I mean that," he said, hands in his pockets as he paced near the console table against the far living room wall. "Do you think someday you'll take down some of these pictures of you and Patrick?"

I wiped my hands on a stray dish towel, slowly walked toward the jackass, and stood frozen in the arch between the kitchen and living room, staring at him.

"I don't mean get rid of them...just so there's less of them displayed, is all I'm wondering...when you're ready, of course."

"I swear to God, Adrian, if you ask about him again...if you have Dom snooping around...," I said firmly, knowing I'd caught him off guard.

"You'll what?"

"I'll break up with you."

"You wouldn't." He winked.

"I would," I said, stone-faced.

"I wouldn't let you."

"I'd move, and you'd never find me." I couldn't help but grin this time.

"Oh...," he said, grabbing me at the waist. He pulled me toward him and kissed below my ear. "I'd find you," he whispered. "Maybe not at first. But I'd find you."

"And what if I asked you to leave me alone?"

"Maybe I would, maybe I wouldn't...but I'd always know where you were."

"Because you love me so much?"

"Because I love you so much," he said. Then he added, "You know why I did it..."

"And you know why I don't like it."

"I'm sorry."

"No you're not."

"You're right, I'm not."

"No stone unturned, I get it," I said, unaware of how soon I'd turn over a truth that could never be unknown.

FIFTEEN

Adrian

THIS LIFESTYLE WASN'T learned, at least not in the way of typical learning. A learner often begins with little to no knowledge and gradually assimilates to a place of insight. What I knew about this life did come gradually, but I was never an outsider. I was a product of the surroundings I was born into, and I was wise to remind myself of that. I acknowledged that most people wouldn't understand my life because of what they themselves were born into. Not everyone would agree with my day-to-day, and that was fine.

As a child, I noticed the way outsiders would sometimes look at my father like he was some kind of monster. They knew who he was, and yet they didn't really know who he was. I didn't understand it; to me he wasn't a criminal. But now, as an adult, I knew that it took all kinds of people to make this globe spin around, and although people of the underworld were particularly marginalized and misunderstood, there was no other group for me. I belonged in this world and not much could make me feel bad about that.

Time and experience change your perspective. I didn't mind being seen as an animal, because at this stage in my life, I knew that I was wolf. The wolf and the wiseguy share a lot in common. The wolf gets a bad rap, always has, but in the end, he is feared and always will be. I'd rather be feared than keep a golden reputation, and like the wolf, my life expectancy wasn't great.

Wolves are expected to live about twelve years, but many only make it to four or six because they die of starvation. They have those nasty, deadly teeth, and they die of starvation? It doesn't make sense until you understand that wolves like to hunt animals much larger than themselves, often up to ten times their own size. You have to imagine a wolf capable of finding something, anything, just to stay alive. But *no*, the wolf says, *I hunt giants*—have to respect the wolf for that.

Regular people tell stories like "Little Red Riding Hood" and love to talk about the wolf in sheep's clothing. Like I said, bad rap, but in all honesty, it made my job easier. I didn't get hung up on the fear-induced tales others told; I was just happy they were giving me the fear I deserved. I didn't care about their stories; I was too busy making my own. My stories were real, and although they put me at risk to, let's just say, die of starvation, in the end, they were my own, and that's something a good number of men don't have.

Most people wouldn't want my life, because I did things that didn't seem human. With my human brain, I often thought like an animal, and that was fine by me. In the end, I'd rather live half an expected life on a wilderness path; I'd rather hunt giants than be human. I'd rather be wolf.

Wolves are all about two things: their pack and their territory. And like the wolf, I'd lay it all down to protect them both. This was a "shoot first, ask later" state of living. I didn't ask permission; I didn't beg for forgiveness. A threat to my pack was eliminated immediately. I pulled the trigger and forced forgiveness wherever it applied, because my job wasn't about "Kumbaya" and making sure precious little feelings weren't hurt. My job was to protect this life and my pack at all costs.

The number one threat to my pack was a rat, or as a layman might say, a wolf in sheep's clothing. I might call it a sheep in wolves' clothing, but anyway, there was nothing lower than a rat. They're a cancer, and like any oncologist worth his weight in dollar bills, my goal was to catch on early. You have to snuff out that disease before it's too late. The nastiest, most severe things these cynical eyes of mine had seen had all been done to a rat. I'd caught a rat; I'd killed a rat; and I'd done it more than once without an ounce of regret.

Back in New York, way back when, this guy Vick came on our crew. He seemed legit, nothing off about him for the longest time. He got kind of close to my family and we did stuff together. He was one of us. I went to the hospital with flowers and a stuffed bear and all that when his daughter was born. Two weeks later, my dad called me in with something serious. Turned out our boy Vick was a bottom-dwelling, scum-of-the-earth, no-good rat, and this ole boy was chosen to do the farewell honors. I felt bad for his wife, of course because Vick was gone but more so because everyone eventually knew her husband died a rat.

Wolves communicate through howling. It's a language only

they can understand, and sometimes these howls get territorial. To the unknowing ear it's a terrifying sound, but to a wolf it's just another day at the office. Even wolves know you've got to change your tone every once in a while. It's how you get things done.

You've got to know how and when to howl, though. You've got to be smart about it, because sometimes wolves will howl for nothing more than to hear their own voices. Street guys will hear this and think it's a rally cry or something. Their appetite is wet all because a random wiseguy needed to blow some steam, and before you know it, howls galore. I get it, I do, but it gets out of hand. Expedient does not mean flippant, get that through your head right now. You can't be flippant on the street and expect to keep your head. Some guys never grasp this.

It's like the time my friend Louie came in and told all the guys he just beat the daylights out of his annoying neighbor. It got a good laugh; the guy had a knack for storytelling, but what he didn't have was long-term sense. He beat this guy and got the boys riled up. Within twenty-four hours, one guy had decided on divorce; another had kicked his unruly teenager out of the house; and finally, a third had shot and killed a tollbooth worker after she shorted him fifteen cents—all because Louie decided annoying people were disposable and the rest of us decided it was funny. Friggin' Louie and his unnecessary howl.

To make matters worse, the tollbooth worker ended up being some mobster's niece, so he took it pretty personally. Word got around; our two families met; and the decision came down: our guy was on the chopping block, and we had to let this mob uncle do the offing. Somebody, probably a friend, had to drive him to this shady bar on the far side of town and let him get shot. Carelessness will get you killed.

Wolves, like wiseguys, don't know the word *moderation*. A

wolf, maybe a hundred pounds, will eat twenty pounds of meat in one sitting. That's some rowdy overindulgence right there. Give a wiseguy a $100,000 score? He'll blow it all and then some in a single weekend. Booze, babes, and bad decisions make the money go bye-bye. We'll never step foot in Vegas again, we say on the plane ride home, but we all know it's a lie. I went to Vegas in debt and came home in more debt. I went with loads of cash and came home with a debtor on my back. It takes a while to learn, and some never do. Maybe it's because there's no one to really tell us, because all the old, smart guys are dead. Maybe it's because tigers don't often change their stripes. Either way, I once was a tiger, but I became more of a leopard. I didn't like owing anybody or being owned. I liked having options; there's freedom in that.

The wolf is all about the hunt. He not only hunts in the pack, he lives in the pack. It's the same for us, and like the wolf, I lived a life of hierarchy rooted in a hard-and-fast set of laws. It's tradition. It's nature. It's the way of the alpha male and, as always, he leads the pack. The wolf has his boys, sure, but do you know who makes him really hunt? His mate. She stays closest. She hunts with him; she gives him his pups. There's not much this chosen wolf can't do. It was the same with Julia. She came along and joined my pack, made me a better hunter, all while proving Adrian De Luca had a beating human heart after all.

God, she made everything better. The way she acclimated to my life happened more perfectly than I could have ever hoped. It astounded me. She was an angel—an angel who became my secret weapon, it seemed. She was different than all the other wives and girlfriends, but they loved her, kind of looked up to her in a way. It was surprising at first, because I'd originally just thrown her in the mix with very little help and expected her to be eaten alive. Out of shock and awe, she was, but it lasted only a second and then she just sort of blossomed. It was like she'd found her calling and stepped right into it. It was weird.

These street girls found themselves endeared to my Julia, a classic, put-together woman, who not only looked and sounded educated but was herself an educator. My guys came to work saying their wives just loved her, couldn't say enough good things about her. This was odd, because these women were always up for a bad word. You think you've heard it all, but never with these women.

The alpha male wolf typically only mates with the alpha female, and after intercourse, they remain hooked together for a half hour. Although this poses a threat to their safety, the alpha male is saying, *hey everybody, this piece belongs to me, and the only pups she'll be having are mine, okay?* And sure, there's the love thing, the romance, but again, he's sort of marking his territory. I felt the same way about Julia. She made everything in my life better, and I wanted to make her totally mine before she got wise and ran the other way.

Buying the ring was easy—huge, sparkly diamond, which was mostly for me—and hey, we were good to go. What woman would turn that down? Well, Julia might've, which is why I almost pulled my hair out over the proposal. I spent hours and hours trying to come up with the perfect thing, but every idea I thought was great seemed like something Julia wouldn't like—typical for us, I guess.

I wanted to get sentimental but I had to do it big. Anyway, I called in a favor, spent a truckload of cash, and told Julia to dress nice, and she did, which is why she was confused when our limo stopped at the entrance to Wrigley Field. There wasn't a game. In fact, the Cubbies were out of town playing the Mets—again, typical Julia and me—so it was just us, a partially lit stadium, and however many workers it took to pull off a romantic hot dog and nachos dinner at home plate.

Julia was enjoying herself, and I could tell she wanted to say something but knew what was coming, so she just sat in delight, trying to keep her outfit—as expensive as it was white—clean. "I could have sworn they said there would be chicken wings. Want me to ask?"

"Adrian, I'm stuffed in this dress. What do you want me to do? I can't fit one more thing."

"You're right, you're right...I'm sorry," I said, realizing I was actually starting to get a little breathy. I sent a signal and, within the minute, we had fireworks and, as planned, *Julia* written in cursive across the jumbo screen. She didn't even notice; I had to point it out. And when she turned to look back at me, I was holding the ring.

She grinned, allowed me to slip it on her finger, and said, "You could have just asked, you know."

We went home and changed clothes. Then we walked to Lydia's, because Julia wanted a milkshake. When I caught her admiring the diamond, she looked up and asked, "So did you steal it?"

"Does it matter?"

"Would you answer the question?"

"I bought it," I said truthfully, which she seemed to appreciate. "Would you change your mind if I hadn't?"

"I'd like to think I would." She grinned.

SIXTEEN

Julia

WE DECIDED ON a wedding date and compromised when it came to the schedule of events. I would have been content with the courthouse steps on a random Tuesday afternoon, but Adrian would have none of it. I'd already gone through the hoopla of a traditional wedding ceremony, not to mention the fact that my mother didn't even know I was dating, let alone betrothed. I couldn't very well submit an engagement photo to the hometown newspaper, not that many people still do that.

I appeased Adrian by agreeing to a simple park wedding late in the evening and a nice dinner with our friends afterward. It seemed a perfect meet in the middle, but the closer we got to the wedding, the more extravagant Adrian's additions to the plan became.

Before I knew it, we were renting a multimillion-dollar estate outside the city limits. It looked like a French chateau right from the cover of a luxury magazine, and even the backyard, where we'd have the ceremony, was so stunning I could hardly protest. The reception would be held inside, in the Grande Salon—an oversized living room, although to call it that is laughable, because it's really more of a ballroom—that opens up to a magnificent stone terrace overlooking the back of the property.

Adrian gave me $30,000 and said, "Here baby, go get your dress and have fun. Don't forget the shoes...and the veil thingy. You know what, you'll need more." And he forked over another $10,000 as if he'd found a stray five-dollar bill.

"Just how much do you think a veil thingy goes for these days?" I asked.

"I don't care, just get the one you want. And let me know if you need more dough. Don't even look at the tag, Julia, I mean it, just pick one."

What the...but why was I even the least bit surprised?

The thing I resented most about getting married a second time was that it forced me to compare everything to the way it had been the first go around. In many ways, life with Adrian was more convenient, and exciting of course, due in large part to his lavish attitude toward money and, really, life in general.

My first wedding was nice but economical, and my parents had been wise to set aside a specific budget years before I would ever need it. Patrick and I had been given permission to use the money however we wanted, and we decided to put part of it toward a down payment on a house. We never regretted the choice, but it meant that, when it came to things like choosing a wedding dress, I was a bit limited. I didn't even try on the one I knew I wanted, because it was far too expensive. The dress I chose was pretty, but I'd be lying if I said I didn't think about the other one almost every time I saw the wedding photos. It was such a trivial thing to hold on to, but I did, and I think what really bothered me wasn't the dress but rather the knowledge that a person can truly have the most important dreams come true but still have to give up a part of their wish list.

That's a harsh reality no matter how minor the things being let go, and maybe I wasn't letting the dress go since it was never mine in the first place. Maybe I was just sitting on my hands as it floated by. Maybe that's what stung—letting it drift away, sure I'd never see it again. The expensive wedding dress had passed me by a decade prior, but it came back around, and who would've thought?

I was born a saver, not a spender, and it couldn't have hurt that my father had been the president of our local East Bank and Trust. But Adrian eased me into being more comfortable with spending money. He'd buy me expensive gifts and I'd squirm in discomfort, and he just kept it up without saying a word. But then, around the time we were engaged, he sat me down and said, "Listen, Julia. I've worked hard to be able to buy these things for you. If you don't enjoy them, at least smile and pretend to be excited. Just let me enjoy it."

I asked if he ever worried about the future.

"No," he said very bluntly.

"Neither do your guys, apparently."

"What does that mean?"

"Well...I always know when things are going well at work. You're all busy, busy, and then there's a jackpot followed by an enormous, unjustified spending spree, and then some of those same guys are out the next week looking for a loan."

"What do you know about my guys?"

"More like *who* I know: their wives. Adrian, I've given them groceries."

"What's really your point?"

"I don't want to live like that."

"You won't have to."

"How can you make that promise? Funny, I didn't know they offered 401(k)s in your line of work."

He got a good chuckle out of that one and went on to explain his stance on 401(k)s. "What I have is better than that travesty of a plan," he said. "Julia, we're set, don't worry."

"How set?"

"Way more than a 401(k)."

"What do you mean *way* more?" I asked.

"A stack here, a stack there...and I've got a big stack on the way."

"On the way..."

"Yeah, I'm glad you brought it up."

"I don't think I was the one who brought it up." But he ignored me, pressing on, of course. Adrian always presses on.

"I'll take it offshore, somewhere clean, maybe in your name if that's okay? No one could touch it."

"Why in my name?"

"Just an extra precaution. In case something happened to me, which it won't."

"Or to hide it from the Feds..."

"That too."

"Don't you think they would know to look for it under my name?" *Why am I legitimately participating in this conversation?*

"They would. But maybe we wouldn't use *your* name. Maybe I'd get you some documents under a different name, and we'd go on a little trip, get the account all set up."

"Adrian!"

"What? It's not a big deal. You would never get caught. My guy's legit."

"Is this why you want to get married as soon as possible, so I can be your little accomplice?"

"Technically we wouldn't have to be married to pull this off."

"Not the point."

"Come on, baby, I'm only telling you this because I trust you, and I'm only doing this to set us up for life. *Us.*"

"And then what? You're just done?"

"Of course not."

"So why…" I trailed off, unsure of whether to continue.

"Why what?"

"Nothing."

"You can say it. It's fine. I think I know where this is headed."

"You think so?"

"You wanna know why I'd keep doing this work if I don't *need* the money."

"Something like that."

"Why take the chance is what you're saying."

"That's exactly what I'm saying."

"I don't know, what else would I do?"

"Anything, you could do anything."

"What, go to school or something? Learn to paint? Take up beekeeping?"

"Raise a family. Take your future wife on an extended vacation." I winked.

"I take you places all the time."

"Well yeah, but…there's always something on your mind with

work...and the stress. And the chance...you know, that something could go wrong."

"Jules, I ain't going to jail."

"What about getting hurt? You could die. You know that's my worst fear...for *good* reason."

"We're all gonna die sometime."

"And you're just so nonchalant about it."

"Sure, I think about it, but so does everyone. It's life, and it's how this lifestyle works."

"But do you think you could ever quit?"

"The life? Altogether?"

"Yes."

"Hmmm...it's called *the life* for a reason. It's not a job or just a paycheck. It's been my life," he said, and it made me think about his family.

"You still didn't answer the question...or maybe you did."

"Jules...I don't know what you want me to say...it feels sacrilegious to even think about it."

"I don't want you to say anything specific. I'm just asking."

"Okay. That's good. I don't know how to explain it. I just...it's who I am."

"I know," I said calmly, accepting what he said as a truth I already knew. It wasn't news to me that the totality of Adrian's identity was being a gangster. It was the center of his life. I knew he loved me, like really, really loved me, but sometimes I wondered about my place in his world.

We'd changed little things about each other, but the dramatic changes belonged to me. I was the one who'd practically abandoned my friends. I was the one about to quit my job. I, not Adrian, had budged and blurred a preexisting view of wrong and right and perfected the ability to look the other way. My lifestyle was the one that had changed so drastically, and it was my world, upside down as it may have been at the time, that was tilted and twirled and shaken like a snow globe before I could even think to give consent.

Sure, Adrian cursed less frequently at my request. I'd been led to truly believe he was now a one-woman man, which I knew wasn't always the case. His late nights were less and less frequent. But other than that, not much about his life had changed, and there were things about Adrian that would never change. He had such a thirst for the life he lived. He was a good man occasionally willing to do "bad" things. But still, he wanted the house and the wife and the cars and the kids. He wanted security for his family but danger for his spirit, and Adrian was one of the few people on this planet who could make the two coexist.

Adrian knew there were scores to be won and believed himself worthy of winning them. It was a treacherous, smarts-imperative life, and even though Adrian had given me an honorable place in it, I wondered about its longevity.

"Do you love me because of who I am or in spite of it?" he asked, holding me.

"Both." It was complicated, but I said it simply.

"Perfect answer." He smiled.

"This is who you are. I get it. Your job is at the heart of everything you do...so what about me? Where am I?" I asked, looking forward to what he might say, and his answer did not disappoint.

"If what you say is true...that my job is the heart, well... you're here making it beat."

"Such a corn dog," I teased, but hearing him say it was happiness.

The mob was in his blood, and not even I would be able to

wash that away from him. There was a part of me that wanted to, as any sane woman would, but at the end of the day, I loved all of Adrian and he made me feel safe.

That was the part that should have scared me—that he was so dangerous, and yet I felt so safe, like nothing bad would ever happen to me again.

SEVENTEEN

Adrian

IT DOESN'T MATTER who you are or what you're fit to do; you're constantly giving or taking tests, whether you realize it or not. In some relationships, these tests come by way of politics or religion, and a person can pass or fail with nothing more than a single glance.

Oh, you're a Republican? Are you at least a cool Republican? Is it because of taxes? Are you rich? At what age do you consider baptism essential? How much or how little water are you convinced to use, and if someone gets the measurements wrong, if the water isn't holy enough, do you believe an eternity in hell will or should be the punishment? Relationships have been cut short, or never begun, all because the person of interest roots for the wrong sports team. My point is this: Be careful what you share about yourself.

What a person says is important, but actions reveal all. I always let people gab all they wanted, didn't make any final decisions about them right away, not even if their words were music to my ears. This was because I knew that something would eventually happen, something that would force an immediate, authentic reaction on their part, and this reaction would serve as my decision point. The most crucial part of show-and-tell has always been *show*, so if they screwed up on the *show*, they might as well have thrown *tell* out the window.

Julia was always straightforward with me. She answered my questions honestly and rarely refrained from saying something that might have seemed opposite of what I wanted to hear. She was upfront about who she was, what she was thinking, what she feared. I liked that, and it was a bonus that I loved all of her answers, even when they didn't line up with mine.

She aced that area with flying colors, but like everyone else, there was something more to know about her, something I always knew and, for the first time in my life, because I loved her so much, dreaded. Julia was, almost to a fault, honest and righteous, so I worried her morality would prevent her from passing the test I knew would eventually, in one way or another, arrive. How she reacted to this test would determine everything, and the name of this test was *loyalty*.

Ask me my favorite word. Ask me what I valued above all else. Ask me what I built a life and a fortune on. Ask me the most important virtue in a person. It's loyalty. The measure of a man, the promise of how far he can go in life, is in direct proportion to the way he can truly answer these two questions: 1) Are you a loyal man?; and 2) How loyal are the people closest to you?

Take my limbs, take my money, but for God's sake, don't breathe disloyalty anywhere near me. If I didn't have loyalty, I was a dead man, so to me, trust was the ultimate currency.

When you want to know if a person is loyal, let them be tested, but don't always be the giver of the test. You can, sure, but I don't think it's the most effective way. When I was getting to know a new guy, there was only so much vetting my crew and I could do on our own. But eventually something happened, something out of our control, and we found out who a person really was. The result was an answer more pure than any outcome we could have finagled on our own. That's what I loved and hated about this life.

I hated that we could break our backs for months and plan for every little detail, but something stupid and insignificant could come along and tear the whole plan to shreds. I'd seen guys imprisoned, shot, or put in the ground all because of something as random as a little girl walking her dog across the street. Traffic jams had literally cost me thousands. Timing's a real beast, but sometimes it comes along and saves you.

Other people, even your enemies, can solve problems you didn't know you had and, on a great day, put the doubts you wish you didn't have to bed. I don't know if it's karma or just the name of the game, but whatever it is, I learned to embrace it.

When one of my guys got a new girl, I was a mixture of pleased and paranoid. The plus side of my guy having a steady girl was that I only had one of them to worry about as opposed to a random string of prostitutes and one-night stands. One good woman made a lot of my worries about a guy go away and, on the other hand, had the potential to create new problems. Good food and good sex on the regular keeps a guy from fidgeting. Fidgeting leads to spinning wheels, and spinning wheels lead to fighting, and while a guy wanting to fight was someone I could often put to use, restlessness leads to carelessness, which always wound up being just one more headache for ole Adrian.

Women solved a lot of my problems, but when my guys got serious about a new one, I prayed she wasn't a coke addict, in need of constant attention, or the type that got her rocks off by starting petty arguments. Was she cool with the lifestyle? Did she look good when we went out in groups but not so put-together as to make me think she could be a cop? And most importantly, did she know the meaning of the word *discretion?* Great, I'd still do my due diligence and double check, as I'd always done with women of my own—especially if I thought they were gonna hang around for a while. I'd have them followed. I'd use my resources to dig as deep as I could. It was no different with Julia, and even though she found out and didn't like it, I was still glad I did it.

There wasn't a sleazy thing about Julia, but she never acted like she was better than anyone in my crew—and God knows, she was better than every single one of us. She didn't have much in common with the other women, but she got along with them, even inspired them, I think. They liked her a whole lot, and that's really saying something.

Julia was the epitome of class, but I knew she wasn't a cop. It wasn't because I'd been to her school and heard years-old stories from her coworkers but because I knew she didn't have it in her. She was missing that element of hardness, so much so that not only was she not a cop or a Fed, but I could guarantee she never even *thought* about being one. Jackpot.

I'd found the perfect woman, and maybe it wasn't so convenient that she was a widow to a man she truly, truly loved, but even that fact was slightly encouraging. The only thing left to know was, would she talk? The universe came along and presented her with a question I never could have asked as seamlessly. She got the test, and I got my answer.

EIGHTEEN

Julia

ADRIAN BROUGHT THINGS to my life that I never imagined experiencing, let alone even needing to think about. It wasn't just the obvious ones, like illegal gambling and strip clubs, guns with scratched-off serial numbers, and the ever-looming threat of "getting whacked." It was a lightning-bolt moment the first time I heard someone use that term, a sort of record player screeching pause to my stream of consciousness where I couldn't avoid asking myself, *is this real life?* It was, and I decided, just like I'd done with the major issues, that I was fine with it.

But there were small things I hadn't accounted for, things I couldn't dream of because I didn't have the capacity to know them until I saw each one right before me.

There was the night Dom came to my house cupping one hand tightly over the other. Blood was dripping, and as he stepped inside, the entry light exposed a nice, even layer of crimson splatters along his neck. I hadn't expected to see something like that, hadn't said I was willing to participate until I readily, and without question, led him to the laundry room utility sink. We got him cleaned up; I pulled a bottle of liquid stitches from the bathroom medicine cabinet; and when it was all said and done, Dom went on his way with a handful of brownies I'd baked just before his arrival.

It wasn't until I lay in bed that night that it occurred to me how unfazed he'd been. I opened the door and there he stood, breathing normally. He didn't look over his shoulder or act in a rush. He wasn't worried or interested in offering an explanation in the least little bit. It was just normal to him—and apparently now, to me.

Once, not long after my dad passed, I went to Fancy's to drop Adrian some lunch. Through the cracked office door, I saw two blonde bombshells sitting before him, completely naked except for tiny, bejeweled thongs. A hint of something, not quite jealousy but close, crawled into my chest, my gut, but quickly vanished. I heard Adrian say, "So anyway...we'll make sure that guy never comes back. What a piece of trash." I knocked casually, walked in, and all three of them turned and smiled. "Hey Jules," one of the girls said. "Oh, that smells good. I'm so hungry," the other said in regard to the bag of food in my hands. Adrian got up from his chair and planted a huge kiss square on my lips, and the girls left.

Never did I imagine being fine with two beautiful, naked strippers having a private meeting with my man. Never did I think

I'd want someone who had never filed a legitimate tax return. Never had I imagined being linked to questionable activity, and certainly never did I envision being questioned by the authorities. But all of it did eventually happen.

Adrian and I were eating dinner at Lydia's. It was a few weeks after the engagement, so we were busy because of the excitement and also because business was especially complicated for Adrian, or so it seemed, as always. He received an urgent call, said he had to leave, and kissed me before darting out the door. It wasn't all that unusual, and I wasn't upset, at least not until a few minutes later when a woman about my age appeared.

I recognized her from the diner. She'd been there before but never sat especially near. On this night, she'd been reading a newspaper in the back corner. She was sort of attractive but a little plain and seemed well put-together. She wore a pantsuit and sensible heels, and once she slid into the place Adrian had just been sitting, I figured out why. "Hi Julia." She flashed a legitimate badge before I could react in the slightest. "Special Agent Bradshaw." *Shit.*

"Am I in some sort of trouble?" I asked, casually setting my napkin on the table.

"I don't know, are you?"

"Not to my knowledge," I answered, trying to sound innocent, but maybe it was a little too innocent.

"I'll make this brief, Julia." She leaned in. "There's an investigation going on, and Adrian is right in the center of it. Which reminds me, now where are my manners? Congratulations on the engagement," she deadpanned. "You know, I'd hate to see your life implode on account of a thug like him."

"Excuse me?"

"Oh, you didn't know he was a thug?" she asked sarcastically.

"I know you're sweet and squeaky-clean, but really...I expected more from you, Julia."

"Agent...Bradshaw, is it?" She nodded that it was, but we both knew I was trying to sound tough. "Is there a point? My soup's getting cold."

"There is. There certainly is...you see, I'm giving you a choice. You'd be an incredible help to our investigation, and in exchange for said help, we'll give you protection and immunity."

"Protection from what?"

"Ms. Hamilton, you need to understand that when all of this implodes, and it will, there's no telling how far the shock waves will go. You're too close, too involved to not be held under a microscope. Your soon-to-be husband is going to prison, and so could you. Unless of course, you cooperate."

"I don't know what you're talking about."

"Oh, sure you do."

"I certainly do not."

"Has he trained you to say that?"

"No."

"What's the bruise on your forehead? Did he do that to you?"

I couldn't speak for laughing. I'd been running in a wooded park a few days before, tripped over a tree root, and gone flying across the path, landing on my face.

"What's so funny about domestic abuse?"

"Adrian doesn't beat me. It was a running accident."

"A running accident. Oh. That makes total sense. You know, I have friends that are runners and they've had a few setbacks... sprained ankle, pulled groin, but never a bump on the head, Julia."

"It's fine if you don't believe me. This conversation is over."

Just then, her face changed. I turned, and there, standing over my shoulder, was Adrian.

"Forgot my wallet," he said, staring a hole through my table guest.

"I was just leaving. Nice catching up with you, Julia. What has it been, ten years?" Was she seriously trying to pull this off? She walked away and out the door, and Adrian, seeing red, sat down again.

"Fed. She's a Fed, right?"

"Yup."

"What did she say?"

I told him everything and he leaned back, running his fingers over the top of his head. "Shit. Shit, shit, shit. Effing Mickey. This is his fault, I know it."

"It'll be fine though, right?"

"I'll handle it, don't worry. And you're sure you didn't say anything else? Not a peep more than what you just told me?" he asked, reaching across the table for my hand.

"Not a word."

He seemed relieved, but his wheels were turning.

"Did I do good?" I asked, nervous.

With a squeeze of my hand, he winked. "You did good, baby."

NINETEEN

Dominic

ADRIAN AND JULIA'S wedding couldn't have come at a worse time, but he was determined to pull it off. Business was overly hectic and I think he thought if the Feds knew he was planning such an event, they'd question just how underwater he felt. And let me tell you, Adrian was in hot water, not that he'd admit it.

Planning the jewelry heist, dealing with Mickey's constant annoyances, and putting out the fires started by sloppy members of our crew, on top of our normal routine, had Adrian and me exhausted. It was like every single day for a month we'd just look at each other and shake our heads, wondering if it was a full moon or something. It wasn't the moon, but we sensed a shifting tide.

Change is constant, but this specific time in history felt different. Something bigger was happening, a movement, a tipping of the scales.

Adrian and I had always been good at rolling with change, but now it felt like we were more interested in fighting for things to stay the same. The outside world was also changing, and boy did we feel the impact.

Modern ways bring pros and cons, but the surge of recent technology made me feel more and more like a dog chasing my own tail. The Feds had never known so much about us, and now, not only were they watching and listening, but they felt they had enough evidence to put together an official investigation to take us down. Adrian and I had long been a circus act of spinning plates, but now we spent equal time as clowns obsessing over government bugs and eyes in the sky. It was nothing new; it's just that our usual awareness had turned to paranoia.

We swept for bugs constantly, and there was a period of time we actually let one stick around a while so we could feed it worthless information. One day we even wore disguises and left Fancy's through the front door. While we were at an important meeting, Adrian's desk was playing a two-hour-long recording we made at my friend Milo's studio.

Drugs became another daily cancer. My dad never had a problem moving them, but there was a no-use policy for his crew. It was strict but not zero tolerance, and you have to keep in mind that the drugs of his day were different than what's on the streets now. He once found out one of his guys was using, so he brought the guy to our house for a detox. The guy was sitting in our formal living room, sweating on my mother's brand new velvet love seat, and I watched him call his wife at my father's insistence. "Hey baby, I'm going on a work trip," he said, telling her he'd see her in a week or less. At the end of the week, my dad sent him home with a stack of cash, maybe as an alibi, maybe as a bribe, but either way, he told him, "Listen. Valentina won't sober you up next time. If it happens again, I'll be the one gettin' you right, you understand?" He must have, because from then on the guy never touched anything more than a cigarette.

Adrian and I could never do that. Some of our members started using and we couldn't help any of them, not for lack of trying but because drugs had become more and more addictive. My mother weaned a guy off of cocaine—*cocaine!*—in a week and he never went back, but I've got guys overdosing in the back lot of the warehouse two days after graduating rehab.

Adrian instituted a new policy: We find so much as donut powder on your lapel, you're done, no questions asked. He didn't mean fired; he meant dead. We'd already gotten rid of members who became bad for business, and you'd think that would have been enough to warn the others, but no. Adrian finally sold our portion of the drug territory, which lessened the problem a bit, but we were still running into addicts on almost every job we did. I'd say we even missed out on $200,000 in gambling debts because our bookies kept finding people overdosed or dead from a bad batch of heroin. Like I said, a cancer.

Greater access to higher education thinned our recruiting pool, and to top it off, wiseguys had never been dumber. I mean, they call it street smarts for a reason, but I wasn't seeing a whole lot of smarts.

So anyway, the wedding stuff really got under my skin. Adrian said it would be a great cover, that the heist would never fall back on us if we planned it for the night of the wedding. I agreed it was a fantastic idea, but to me, it was happening too fast and beginning to spin out of control. I didn't like getting Mickey in on the plan, but it was the only way to pull it off and still give every single member of our crew an alibi.

Adrian kept saying it would all work out and that the score would be good for the family, but I wasn't so sure. There was too much going on, and he should have been strictly focused on keeping us out of the pen, but no, he was also invested in this matrimonial BS. And maybe I wouldn't have been so bitter about it had I not realized my own feelings for Julia—feelings I originally stifled, but it didn't stick.

I'd suppressed plenty throughout my life, which in this line of work is imperative for survival. But the problem with suppressing is that some of the things you're trying to shove into oblivion eventually resurface in a less than ideal way.

The first time I killed a man, I didn't know what to do with myself. I was messed up but confused, because here were these guys I'd admired since I was knee-high slapping me on the back and reaching for celebratory shot glasses. They were the same guys who cheered about my first stolen car, the same ones who came to bail me out of jail when I was only a teen. In those instances, I felt proud of myself, welcome even. But after the murder, I didn't know what to feel.

It took me three days to fall asleep, because I saw the guy's face every time I closed my eyes. I killed him; I knew he was dead, but he found me in my dreams. It was the same reel every time: I was shoveling dirt into his grave and when the job was almost done, his arms poked through, then his head, and then he sat up and stared, saying, "My wife. My daughter. Tell them I'm sorry. Tell them I love them." I'd jolt awake in a cold sweat and wonder what the hell kind of a person I was.

But the stifling got easier with time; I got better at it. Some guys will tell you their number, but not me. Honestly, I forgot a lot of them—not who they were or why they had to get dead, but what it had to do with me. I remembered where they were buried or what street some poor schmuck found 'em on, but they stayed there and I moved along with my life, on to the next thing, brought to me courtesy of time and experience. If only it were all that easy.

When Adrian first came to Chicago, I saw it as a stand-up thing for my dad to take the guy under his wing and had no idea we'd become such fast friends. If I was somewhere, Adrian was there too, and vice versa. He became the brother I never had, and I the one he'd lost; I just never imagined he'd take my place.

It was like I didn't exist anymore, like my father still had one son, and his name was Adrian. It's all the man could talk about, and then, after Adrian had been in Chicago about five years, the books opened up. This was a big deal, because when the books come open, it means someone can get made, and being made means you're set—no more being a foot soldier, and your place in the family is secure because no one can kill a made man without permission from the boss. It's a huge to-do that comes with more responsibility but also more money and a boatload of respect.

The books had been closed several years, but the deaths of several high- and mid-ranking members finally brought the need to open them again. It's just that only one person would be chosen. There was a lot of chatter about who that person would be, and most people naturally assumed I would be chosen, since my father had significant pull and the person who got made would basically be his replacement.

But my father didn't pick me. He made Adrian and never said a word to me about it.

I always felt at home as Adrian's right hand, and I know it's where I belonged, but there was a lot of stifling going on back when it was all still fresh.

The truth was that Adrian and I were an equal amount of skill and smarts, but he was always at the top of his game. He was quick and composed, and he came to this city a man on fire with nothing to lose. It's hard to compete with that, not that I ever really tried, and I accepted that Adrian was one of those guys the universe just loved to shine on. I wasn't born with that energy. It was fine by me. At the end of the day, I liked myself and loved Adrian enough that our friendship never suffered.

We trusted each other with more than just our lives, and I'm not sure who bailed the other out more times. It didn't matter; we never kept track. Fast forward a decade and he was trusting me to take care of Julia when he couldn't be around. He would've done the same for me, except—and maybe this is where the self-loathing came into play—he wouldn't have fallen for my girl the way I did his.

Julia and I were buds from the beginning. She knew what I meant to Adrian and I knew it by the way she looked at me. She treated me like I was important before she even got to know me. She didn't idolize Adrian the way most people did, but you could tell she was always thinking of ways to plain love him, and perhaps the best way she found was to simply let him be himself. Their relationship flourished because of it.

I liked the way she laughed at punch lines that weren't that funny and that she got the jokes some of the other ladies in the group often missed. Walking into her house was like coming home. She'd wait on you hand and foot but then, the next second, plop on the couch and remind you there were cookies in the jar and the kettle was ready to go if tea sounded good. Tea never sounded good to me, but I'd drink it every day if that's what Julia wanted. It was sometimes just the two of us in the car and I'd pretend we were a real thing. I'd shake it off and remind myself that what I was thinking was wrong, but it didn't matter. I was dating a girl named Melanie but fell in love with Julia.

I didn't want, plan for, or welcome it, but it happened, and everything around me was changing so much that I began to question my lifestyle's longevity. That, combined with the long-term effects of stifling, was just enough to coax me into doing what I did.

It was the night before the wedding, and Adrian asked if I would drive Julia to the hotel. He'd arranged for her to stay in a fancy suite, said he wanted her to wake up feeling like a princess, but if you ask me, I think it was a page from his ego's playbook. Yeah, he wanted Julia to feel special, but more so, he didn't want her sleeping in the bed she once shared with another man. He didn't want her waking up and being reminded of Patrick in any way, so he sent her off to a place less likely to conjure up those old memories.

The rehearsal dinner was over, and I waited outside the restaurant as the lovebirds said good-bye, which took forever. Julia finally got in the car, and I honked the horn at Adrian as we pulled away. He held up a hand, and we drove out of sight to what felt like, to me, a funeral, but Julia seemed to be floating on air.

"Anxious about the big day?" I asked.

"Nope." She smiled.

"Not even a little bit?"

She seemed to consider it but then shook her head. "Weird, huh?"

"Well, you've done this before...maybe it helps."

"Yeah. Maybe so." She smiled. "I thought I'd be nervous...or annoyed. You know, this wedding has been blown completely out of proportion. It was supposed to be simple. He *promised* me it would be simple. But you know Adrian..."

"Yup...sure do."

She laughed, and for a few blocks we didn't speak.

"You know, for a while...after Patrick...I was unsure about everything. *Everything*. But now..."

"You're sure."

"Yeah."

"About what?"

"That it's real. That I love him. That it will work," she said, stabbing my heart with each word. "But what's with the questions, anyway?" She giggled. "Are you thinking about popping the question? Melanie seems really great."

"Yeah, she's...great." We were getting close to the hotel, and I had a decision to make. There was something about Adrian that Julia didn't know but she'd want to, or at least I would. I'd promised myself I would never tell her, because the details were a disaster, and I didn't want her to hate me. But the desire to come clean bubbled over.

Telling her would change everything. It would break her heart and, furthermore, serve as the beginning of the end of my closest friendship. I didn't want that, but I wanted Julia, and this was my one shot at the chance that she might love me in return. It wouldn't happen right away, and I wouldn't ask that she love me the way she loved Patrick, or even Adrian. All I wanted was for her to love me. My father picked Adrian, and Adrian picked Julia. I wanted her to pick me.

Instead of dropping her at the door, I pulled through the overhang and sped back onto the street. "There's something I need to talk to you about," I said, knowing she was puzzled without even looking at her.

"Okay...what?"

"Adrian."

"What about him?"

I didn't know how to even begin. I wanted it to sound as coarse as possible, but I also wanted to soften the blow. I wanted it to hurt her right into my arms, but I didn't want to hurt her. She didn't deserve it, but she deserved to know. "Adrian and I have been friends a long time."

"Yeah..."

"And I love him like a brother."

"Dom, where's this going? If this is part of your best man speech, just save it. Don't make me cry tonight."

"I'm sorry, Julia...I just...I don't want to say it, but I think I should..."

"You're scaring me," she said, already on the brink of tears as we passed one block and then two before I turned the car into a side alley.

"I'm sorry, I'm sorry...I don't want to do that, I..."

"Just spit it out, come on, you're freaking me out."

The choice to tell felt like a mistake, and yet it was my ticket to a new life. Torn and frustrated, I sat in silence. Then I blurted out: "He killed him."

PART THREE

TWENTY

Julia

I KNEW WHO "him" was as soon the word left Dominic's mouth. It seemed the blood had simultaneously rushed to and drained from my face. Dominic looked over at me and, for a moment, our eyes locked, but I reached for the door, flung off my seatbelt, and stepped out onto the crack-filled sidewalk.

I took several paces. Then I stopped, turned around, and watched as Dom got out and stood just in front of the vehicle. "You're saying Adrian killed Patrick?"

He nodded in the affirmative.

"Why? Why would he do that? Why are you telling me this?"

"I just...I don't know. I thought you should know."

"How did he even know him? Did he plan this? Did he come looking for me?"

"Julia, it's not like that. In Adrian's defense, it wasn't like that."

"But you're saying he killed him."

"In essence, yes."

"In essence?"

"It's complicated, Julia. Just calm down."

"Calm down?!" I was sobbing now, and with each step Dominic took toward me, I felt my chest rise and fall as if it might explode. "Get away from me!"

"It was a fluke," he said, taking a step back. He waited for me to settle down and asked if I wanted to know more. I nodded that I did.

"There was this guy, Benny. Pretty good kid until he ran off with some money. All he had to do was pick it up from this store owner down the street and bring it back, but he never showed. Twenty grand. We jumped down the store owner's throat, thought maybe he got rid of Benny, but he got the exchange on video surveillance. Adrian was livid. Vetted everybody, but no one knew anything and we couldn't find him.

"Months go by, and one day, we're out doing some stuff in my car. It's me, Adrian, and two of our guys, and who do we spot walking down the street but Benny. Bastard was dumb enough to come back to town. Maybe he never left, I don't know, but Adrian gets out of the car and beats Benny's face in. It's still daylight and people are on the street, so we drag him around to the back of a building and rough him up some more. He's telling us this sob story that doesn't add up, and he's got track marks all over his arm. Adrian knew he was never getting that money back, so he tells Benny to turn around and, well, you probably know what happens next. Benny's dead."

"Dom. What does this have to do with Patrick?"

"Benny's bleeding out and we turn around, ready to leave, but there's this guy standing at the end of the alley staring at us. He saw the whole thing. We start walking toward him and he turns and leaves. Gave us a look like, hey just go about your business. But Adrian tells me to follow him, make sure he doesn't go to the cops or something. So I do what Adrian said and follow him into a convenience store. Followed the guy for three days."

"You were stalking Patrick?"

"I didn't know who he was...not until the first time you invited me over for dinner."

"Chicken parmesan...Dom, that was months ago."

"I recognized the house but didn't know why until I walked in and saw the pictures...it's why I didn't eat much. Julia, I couldn't...I didn't have a cold. I was sick to my stomach." He was telling the truth; I could tell.

"He never mentioned it...did he go to the police?"

"I saw him talking to an officer. It looked friendly, like maybe they knew each other."

"Mr. Murphy...he lives down the street."

"I don't think he talked."

"Then why did you kill him?"

"Adrian said to scare him. He wasn't supposed to die. The kid was supposed to shoot him in the arm or something, just rattle him. I don't know what happened in that store, but he wasn't supposed to die. The kid never came for his money...he knew he messed up."

"Stop...stop! Stop talking. I don't want any part of this." I cried. "I want out. I'm done. I can't...I can't do this."

"Are you mad?"

"Am I mad?" I scoffed, almost laughing. "I don't know what I am. I was a normal person, and then one day my husband got shot. That's still kind of normal, right? But then...then I meet Adrian and things are not so normal anymore. And now you come along and tell me that my fiancé is the reason my husband got shot...and you ask me if I'm mad? Who am I supposed to be mad at, Dom? Am I supposed to be angry with you that Patrick was followed or with myself for understanding why you did it? What am I supposed to be right now? Who am I?! Who are you?!" I gave his chest a push and turned away.

"I know...I know, Julia. I'm sorry. I just...I meant, are you mad at me?"

"No," I said honestly, knowing that I sort of hated him but couldn't because I knew the lines he was crossing.

"So what are you going to do?"

"I don't know, Dom, what did you expect me to do? What's the protocol for this sort of thing?" My haughty laugh sent his eyes to the ground.

"It's up to you to decide."

"I just want to go home."

"Do you really think he'll let you do that?"

"Then why did you tell me?! What am I supposed to do?" It was the first time in my life that I felt truly hysterical, but Dominic, although upset, was composed. He calmed me down and took me in his arms. My face itched from smeared, dry makeup; my guts seemed to swell and carry disease to every inch of me. I rested against him, my head frozen to his chest. I couldn't blink; I just stared at the side of the building and the mortar that had oozed between its bricks. No one had bothered to scrape it off before it dried, leaving it stuck like that...forever, and I'd have felt stuck if it hadn't been for Dom.

"I'll help you," he said as I nodded along. "We'll get you out of town. I'll make sure you're safe. Okay?"

He drove me to the hotel and saw me to my room. Like he promised, I felt safe, but something entered my mind on the elevator, puzzling me enough to pry. When we reached the door to my suite, I retrieved its key and turned to face him. "Dom, why are you doing this?"

He bit at the inside of his mouth and eventually answered, "Because I care about you, Jules."

It warmed me and worried me. He *cares about me?* I wasn't sure what he meant, but I went on before he could add anything more. "But you're his *best* friend," I pointed out, exhausted.

"Mm-hmm."

"And if he finds out...?"

"He won't. I'll wear the suit, and tomorrow, when you don't show, I'll act surprised."

"So if this works...if you get me out of here without him knowing, and he never finds out...what then?"

"You start a new life and get on with it."

"No, I mean for you. What will you do? Will you stay?"

"Depends."

"On what?"

"You, Julia...it depends on this thing with you."

"Dom..." I shook my head, a lump forming in my throat as I unlocked the door. "This day has been...too much. I need rest."

"Yeah...yeah, let's get you squared away. I'll call you in the morning. First thing."

"Night Dom."

"Goodnight Julia. Sleep well," he said, and I closed the door, happy to be alone, wishing it could stay that way forever, but I watched him through the peephole.

He stood there for a moment and then took off toward the elevator, but halfway there, he stopped and turned around. My heart raced as he reapproached the door, and even more so when he stood in front of it, his face so close to mine. He raised his fist as if he would knock but abandoned his plan at the last second.

He left again and pressed the down button but darted around the corner when the elevator moved too slowly. I couldn't see but heard him burst through the entrance to the stairwell, and when the door slammed behind him, it sounded like the closing of a coffin—I just wasn't sure whose.

TWENTY-ONE

Julia

INSTEAD OF GETTING in bed, I changed my clothes, went to the lobby, and had the concierge call a cab. I needed comfort and wanted to be among my things—and Patrick's old things. Maybe I wanted to say good-bye to them, I don't know.

Each second I spent waiting for the cab found me increasingly overwhelmed with sadness, and it dawned on me that Patrick leaving this earth so suddenly was a blessing. There was no chance to say good-bye to him, and that was, for a long stretch, nothing but a separate and additional dose of grief for me. But tonight I saw it differently. Preparing to say good-bye is overwhelming; I wonder if we get what we need out of it, if it's worth the pain.

I think the best-case answer is sometimes. Sometimes we get closure; sometimes we get a rotten deal; but all the time, when it comes to good-byes, we get pain. Lucky us.

I knew that if I left town, I could never come back, and maybe when I told the driver to take me to my house, I knew we'd never actually get there. Just a few blocks from home, I sat forward in my seat. "Wait. Stop here," I said and got out of the cab.

It wasn't my house I needed to visit. If I never saw it again, I'd still remember every inch. But there was a place I'd never been, one I'd avoided but had visited, if only in my mind, at least a hundred times.

I walked inside it now, smelled its stale, humid air. I roamed the aisles like the owner might after a devastating storm. There had been no tornado or hurricane, but there was destruction written all over that tiny liquor store. Approaching the checkout counter, I searched for the wreckage. I'd heard they repainted the floor, and from the looks of it, the rumors were true. But there, just feet from the register, a puddle-shaped shadow emerged from the medium-grey paint, and in my heart of hearts, I knew it was Patrick's blood stained on the cement underneath.

He was a good man. Compared to Adrian, he was that nice guy down the street. He'd stumbled upon something much different than himself, and it got him killed. Of all the sketchy neighborhoods, of all the less than or mildly suitable foster homes he'd once lived, these walls were the ones to end him? He'd made something of himself. He never dwelled on his negative beginning in life. He was Teflon and made his life different than it could have been.

I was supposed to protect him. I should have never asked him to stop on his way home. I should have noticed a change in his behavior. What kind of wife doesn't notice that her husband has seen a man shot dead? I'd been devoted to him, and who was I to think I could or should or deserved to love someone else? With Patrick, I'd been one woman, and with Adrian, another. Now who was I without either of them?

I'd been carrying a certain element of peace about Patrick's death. It wasn't fair and I was still devastated, but there was an answer that at least made sense: *Wrong place at the wrong time,* I told myself. It happens every day. The story you tell yourself is the navigator of grief, and now, because I'd unknowingly medicated myself with lies, I was lost.

Adrian was supposed to be the guy that changed my story. I thought he'd saved me, but here, all along, he'd been the instigator of my pain, turning an alley I knew nothing about into Patrick's wrong place. Adrian, Dom, and Benny—thieves, each one—were all there. It's just that I couldn't decide which had ultimately stolen the most from me. Benny paid for his sins. Dom offered a penance. But where did Adrian stand in all this? What price would he pay?

"Can I help you find something?" The man behind the counter was rightfully unsure of me.

"I don't think so," I barely answered while grabbing a bottle of Miley's Merlot.

"You doing okay, miss?" he asked, eyes slanted with suspicion, or maybe it was compassion.

"I'm just tired," I admitted, forcing myself to perk up, to smile. Pointing at Patrick's favorite scratch-off game, I said, "Five of those too."

"Feeling lucky?" He winked.

"Not even a little." I handed over the money and walked out the door before he could even begin to prepare change.

I told the cab driver to take me back to the hotel, and without a word, he turned the car around and out onto the street.

Back in the penthouse, I opened the wine, poured a glass, and carried it to the dining room, where I stood hunched over a fancy console. Studying my reflection in the mirrored wall, I noticed my face in a way I never had before. My cheekbones seemed regal. Soft lighting highlighted my jawline, making it appear delicate, altogether feminine, yet somehow strong, resolute. The thin, swollen skin around my eyelashes only showcased my emerald eyes. What did Adrian see when he looked into them? Could I fool him? Could he look at me and see what I wanted him to see, or would he always know exactly what I was thinking?

I made up my mind to find out. I decided to flip the switch, or perhaps it flipped itself. Destiny flipped it—that's what I tell myself now, like I told myself then that this is what was meant to happen. This is what I was meant to do.

So I walked, more like sauntered madly, into the double closet and placed the wedding veil on my head. Again, I stared at myself for a long while, this time in the full-length mirror. Eventually I raised the veil and flipped it over my head. After a refill, I tossed my head back and took three giant gulps of merlot. With a hint of a smile, I raised my glass toward the mirror and clinked a toast to my reflection.

Stay calm, I told myself. It's only a wedding. No, it's a masquerade ball.

Dominic

I cursed myself all the way home. Why did I do that? Why did I tell her I loved her? Well, I hadn't actually said it. But I was trying to. I think I said it without saying it, and maybe that's why I felt the words had returned void.

I didn't know what Julia was thinking, or if she was even thinking about me—probably not. I'd dropped a bomb, and there wasn't time for her to think about me.

Maybe when this blows over, I told myself. *When she gets settled somewhere else, when she's over Adrian and what she thought she had with him, she'll be grateful I was there. He'll be a monster, and she'll remember that I was the guy who exposed him and then saved her from his reach. She could love me—eventually.* I'd be the only one who knew the totality of what she'd been through and we'd bond over never telling another soul.

I'd leave Adrian and slip away without him even suspecting. He'd put the pieces together, of course. He'd have to know I was with Julia—a thought I was ashamed of, but it thrilled me. I didn't want to hurt him but I wanted to beat him, and I guess that's why they say it's a fine line between love and hate. Sometimes I think they're the same.

My mind was spinning—about Adrian, about my mother, about getting Julia out of Chicago. I'd made some calls, constructed a plan. But then my phone rang.

"Hey Dom." It was her. God, she always sounded so good.

"Hey Jules. How are you?"

"I'm okay...hey listen, I've been thinking about tomorrow."

"Yeah, me too. What time are the hair people coming over?"

"Eleven, but—"

"Good, be ready by eight. I'll pick you up at the rear entrance and take you to my friend. He'll drive you out of here and keep you safe. I've got everything you need: phones, credit cards, everything."

"I can't...Dom, I've changed my mind."

My stomach dropped. "Changed your mind? About what?

Julia, you can't stay here. Think of what he did."

"I know what he did. That's why I'm staying. I appreciate the lift, but I have to stay."

"I don't get it. What are you saying?"

"I'm going to marry him."

"Julia..."

"I'm taking him down."

"You can't be serious. It won't work. He'll find out. You can't put yourself through that."

"I need your help."

"I'm trying to give it to you! Be at the door at eight, okay?"

There was a long pause, like she was waiting for me to come around. "Are you going to help me or not? I'm doing this either way, and I swear I won't rat you out, but Dom, I'd like your help."

"Doing what? What can I possibly do? What can *you* do? You can't kill him. You can't hide that from this family," I said, unprepared for what sweet, innocent Julia was about to say.

"You remember that agent?"

"Yeah."

"She wants Adrian bad."

"And you're going to give him to her?"

"Yup."

"It's too dangerous. Julia, you don't know how we handle this shit. They watch us and we watch them. You'll get caught, and he will *kill* you."

"Not if I have your help."

"Julia..."

"Can I count on you or not?"

I paced the apartment, pressing an open hand across my eyes, my nose, my lips. *Shit.* "You can count on me."

"Good. See you at the wedding."

"Yeah...see you there."

"You know what else?" she asked, and I sensed that she was smiling. "He asked if I would open accounts with just my name. Offshore stuff. I told him I'd think about it."

"Yeah?"

"Yeah. I'm gonna do it," she said and hung up the phone.

I'd gone too far. I'd broken the rules. There are things a man just doesn't do because of ethics, things like betrayal and stealing your best friend's fiancée one lie at a time. It's your name and your self-respect on the line. But then there are things men like me get killed over.

Being with another member's wife is punishable by death. Telling non-members our business means a slow and painful death, and doing it over the phone is the most rookie way to go wrong with this rule. If someone accuses you of loose lips or disloyal behavior, deny, deny, deny. But when you know you did it over the phone? You're screwed. There are call logs and taps and a hundred different ways to record anything you want these days.

But Julia trusted me. I was her partner and it felt good. The memory of her voice almost lulled me to sleep, and when morning came, I reminded myself that she and I were a team. Adrian would find out. He always found out. So I'd stay two steps ahead of him. *I trust Julia. Adrian trusts me.* Repeating these advantages to myself brought slight comfort; half a bottle of antacids and a pint of bourbon brought a touch more. *Some best man.*

TWENTY-TWO

Julia

THE WEDDING WAS absolutely stunning, and there's not much else to say about it. Whether it was because of sheer impression or out of a desire to blow smoke up Adrian's rear end, our guests raved over every little thing, not that any of it was little.

I wasn't the person I used to be, so it seemed fitting that no one from my past was there. The only exception was Goldie. She was giddy, like she thought us a fairytale before her very eyes. Good girl falls for bad boy, except this time it was special because it had a happy ending, or so she thought. But this was just the beginning, and seeing her so excited was honestly the only thing that made me feel guilty all day.

I'd woken up that morning with an energy I'd never known;

it was the pulse that would keep me going, the guts I'd need to follow through with the plan. What I was constructing was my own death warrant, but I didn't mind so long as I could use Adrian's blood to sign at the *X*, and I'd drafted this plan with little to no questioning. Nowhere in my being did I think he deserved to be heard.

Adrian was nothing if not meticulous. He had to have known. He had to. There's no way he had a man killed and then married his widow without putting the pieces together. He was too smart, too intuitive. There's no way he saw the man standing at the end of the alley and then, months later, stood in the same man's living room and looked at his picture without realizing who he was. Or maybe he knew all along. Maybe he was checking up on me because he felt bad, and then somewhere along the line, he fell for me. I could believe that scenario. The man had a huge heart but was, at times, the epitome of heartless, so it would make sense.

Regardless of how it all came to be, I woke up on the morning of our wedding thinking about revenge when I should have been thinking about happily ever after. But happiness is what got me in this position to begin with. If I hadn't been so fixated on being happy, I wouldn't be there.

I considered the notion of providence. Maybe the universe was throwing me a bone, giving me the opportunity so many grieving people only fantasize about. I couldn't bring Patrick back, but I could vindicate his death, and that was more than most people can say.

So I did the beauty routine and drank champagne with a few of the girls and the people Adrian sent to do my hair and makeup. This was, of course, after the masseuse arrived to deliver a ninety-minute massage I knew nothing about. *What a flippin' control freak.* It actually made me sick. In another state of mind, I'd find these gifts as thoughtful as the team of spa and beauty professionals certainly thought they were. But there's something about seeing your first husband's blood on a liquor store floor at the hand of your soon-to-be that takes the butterflies away from the romance that could have been.

Anyway, I acted the part, which is the sort of thing I'd never been good at. But to tell you the truth, I'd never felt more powerful than the moment I arrived at the ceremony and stepped out of the limousine. My mindset had me reeling through what seemed an out-of-body experience. It was a nightmare, except I was enjoying it, and the property was a dream.

The trees were lit from top to bottom and along every single branch. The gardening was lush and immaculate, beautiful in every way. Helen hadn't been invited, but she would have died and gone to heaven—you know what, make it hell if I truly have to guess. I'd said the sinner's prayer, so I knew what it entailed, and I just couldn't imagine my mother ever—not even for the Lord—uttering words that implied remorse or admittance of guilt, let alone asking forgiveness.

Slow and deliberate, I slinked to the backyard, turned a corner, and at the music's cue, walked down the lantern-lit aisle to the man I promised my life until death do us part—and I think there was a twinkle in my eye as I said it.

The dinner after the ceremony found Adrian to be the man of the hour, as always, so faking an affinity for being around him hadn't required much effort on my part. Unsurprisingly, it was our private after-hours time together that proved to be a challenge.

I'd prepared with a stiff drink and gave myself a bathroom pep talk as I slipped into lingerie I'd purchased a few weeks prior.

I'd bought it with a completely different intent than the one I now harbored, and remembering it freed a sad tear. It fell to the floor with a single splat, like a dripping sink in an otherwise quiet room. Soft and slow, I swiped my foot across the tile floor, took a breath, and opened the door.

The bed was calling, but I stopped to pour Adrian and myself another drink, and he whistled at me. It would have been sweet, but now, because the tide had turned, I felt like numbered livestock or one of the girls from Fancy's.

Adrian wanted to make love, and I, to keep up appearances, wanted to have sex, and I think we both achieved what we were hoping for. He fell asleep soon after, arm heavily draped over my side, but I, lying in repulsed reflection, found it more difficult to rest.

The past had crashed in on me, and yet it seemed so far away. I wanted to be with my Mr. Shirley. For me, it had always been Patrick, so why did I think life had provided another? How could I have been so naïve in thinking it was Adrian? How could I have believed that the good in him was more than what he let on?

I managed only a little sleep. Then I woke up and, out of a desire to hear something else besides my own run-down thoughts, flipped on the television. I settled on the morning news and curled up in an upholstered chair, barely paying attention to the broadcast until a headline caught my attention.

"A rare jewelry collection was stolen from the Charles Ainsley estate last night. Officials say the thieves got off with a prize worth roughly four million dollars. Mr. Ainsley is offering a hefty cash reward—one hundred thousand dollars—to anyone with information that leads to the recovery of these jewels."

So that's what you've been working on.

TWENTY-THREE

Julia

ALMOST AS IF he'd actually followed a syllabus, Adrian had prepared me to live as a mob wife. Knowledge is power, and because of Adrian, I was enlightened. Because of Adrian, I knew I'd be wise to let Agent Bradshaw come to me.

Every natural instinct told me to seek her out, but it was too dangerous. I couldn't exactly walk into a federal building at will. I couldn't call or even Google her. There were too many things that could go wrong, too many eyes that might see. Or, as Adrian would put it, *you can always count on a coincidence to get you into trouble, but never count on one to get you out.*

Lucky for me, Bradshaw popped up again just two weeks after the wedding. "So tell me, is marriage all it's cracked up to be?"

she asked, sliding into the booth across the aisle. I'd been going to Lydia's alone on purpose, but also because Adrian, like usual, was busy at work. Goldie didn't seem to think much of my more frequent visits, but a trained federal agent might think otherwise, and said agent would be right.

"Oh, it's more."

"Really? How so?"

"You've obviously been watching, so why don't you tell me?"

Agent Bradshaw smiled and waited for a group of patrons to pass. Elbows on the table, she asked, "What do you want, Julia?"

"Oh, I imagine something pretty close to what you want."

"Why the sudden change of heart?"

"I can't say."

"Then why am I here?"

"I have a dentist appointment Thursday," I said, getting up from the table, pretending to be annoyed. "Dr. Shato. Two o'clock."

"Dental health is important." Agent Bradshaw was sarcastic and off-putting, but I needed her, and because I knew she needed me too, I walked out of the diner with confidence—and quite a bit of sass for show.

Agent Bradshaw

Criminals like Adrian De Luca are smart and paranoid but, most of all, relentless. They don't think the way normal people think, and they're willing to go to any extreme to satisfy their need for dominance and control. A person like me keeps this in mind at all times, but the funny thing that happens in a cat-and-mouse game such as this is that sense of self is blurred.

In my quest to take the legs out from under Adrian, I absorbed his own sense of cunning mind games and paranoia. I had to; it was the only way to win; and I was right to walk into this meeting with Julia with rabid caution. What could Adrian have possibly done to push her so far over the edge in such a short time? It felt like a setup. It seemed too easy, but I decided to give her the chance to sell her story, quite frankly because I wanted whatever it was to be real. I wanted Adrian on my scoreboard, and gaining Julia's trust was my golden ticket.

I located the correct Dr. Shato and invaded his office before Julia's scheduled appointment. After a few flashes of the badge and a guise of, "It's probably nothing, but one of your employees is under investigation and we need to take a look around," I was all set up. I wasted time in the restroom and poked around looking for nothing as I waited for Julia to be called back. Her teeth were scraped and polished, flossed and rinsed; meanwhile, across the hall, an unlucky son of a gun found himself the recipient of a root canal. *Ugh, I hate the dentist.*

When the hygienist was through, I slipped into Julia's exam room and shut the door. "We don't have much time," I whispered. "Spill it."

"I'm in."

"Be more specific."

"I'll help you take him down."

"Is he putting you up to this?"

"That's the last thing he would do."

"First time for everything."

"No, it's not like that. He doesn't know...you can't tell him!" I could see she was nervous, full of a fear that can't be faked. "He would kill me."

"Then why are you doing this? What in God's name did he do

to you?"

"I can't say, not here."

"You might have to."

"Listen, I'll get you what you need if your offer is still good."

"What can you get me now that you weren't willing to get two months ago?"

"You and I both know he's in the middle of something big."

"So again, what are you bringing to the table, Julia?"

"I know he was involved in that jewelry heist."

"You *know*? Because we can't find any proof whatsoever."

"I'll find the proof." The way she promised it made me giddy inside.

"Protection. All I can do is keep you safe. But you have to do everything I say, Julia. Don't go off script."

"Okay."

"And you'll have to come in to the office. I have to train you, and—"

"I'm trained, trust me, I'm trained. I'll be fine, just...get him as soon as you can, that's all I ask." I was sure Adrian had coached her until he was blue in the face, and there was something poetic about knowing he'd taught her everything she'd need to take him down. Julia knew about deception, confidence, and the simple but all-encompassing code a mob family lives and dies by, but now she needed to learn my code.

"There are places you'll have to meet me, things you'll have to do. We need to plan this. You have to come in, sign papers, do the federal rigmarole."

She seemed disappointed and I'm sure already going through the logistical reasons something like that would not work for her. "Can't you just...take my word?"

"Doesn't work that way. Sorry, not my rules."

"Fine. When?"

"The movies. Go to the movies." I took out my phone and found a flick Adrian wouldn't want to tag along for. "Show up early, take the emergency exit. I'll be waiting for you. We'll go to the office, do our thing, and you'll be back in that theater before the credits roll, okay?"

"Okay."

"And most importantly, keep up the act with Adrian. Be normal. Smile with teeth. After today, they're nice and shiny," I said, writing my cell phone number on the back of an Invisalign flyer. "You're doing the right thing."

On my way out of the office, I stopped Dr. Shato and assured him there was no reason to be alarmed. "Everyone checks out. Don't go firing anybody," I joked.

"Oh, I feel so relieved." He smiled. *Wonder what that's like.*

Julia did exactly as she was told, and the caution behind our afternoon, however premature, set a nice tone for us both. She was nearly silent in the car but became more talkative once we were in the safe confines of our meeting place: a hotel suite, as opposed to FBI headquarters. Julia seemed to very much appreciate that only a handful of my coworkers knew about the investigation. We questioned her to almost no end about the night of the wedding, but she swore Adrian remained in her sight the entire evening.

"He never left the property, not even for five minutes."

"And Dominic?"

"Same. He made a few calls on his cell phone, but that was it, and they were short."

"Who do you think he was talking to?"

"Honestly, I have no clue. Everyone I can think of was at the wedding."

"But do you know the entire crew?"

"I know everyone Adrian would trust with something this big. I'm telling you, they did it. I just don't know how they pulled it off. Everyone was at the wedding. They must have done it some other time."

"Mrs. Ainsley was home the entire time her husband was out of town, except she left for California Saturday afternoon, and she swears the jewels were still there."

"Maybe she helped them. Maybe they bribed her."

"We're checking into it, but it's starting to look like a dead end. Tell me more about Adrian. What's your relationship like?"

"He doesn't tell me much." Her confession didn't surprise me. *Can't tell what you don't know*—Mob Husband 101. "He knows I'm smart, but he sees me as this innocent angel...and compared to some of the other wives, I am...but I think he gets comfortable around me...he thinks I'll assume the best, not the worst. And he's asked me to do things."

"What things?"

"Open accounts. Offshore stuff. I think he knows where the jewels are, and I think he's going to sell them."

"To whom?"

"I don't know, but we leave for our honeymoon next weekend. The Cook Islands."

"Bingo," I said. "He probably plans to make the sale and deposit the money all in one go. Smart. No getting caught at the airport with all that cash."

"Mm-hmm."

"Don't worry, we'll be watching the entire time. Just do what he says and we'll take care of the rest."

"Okay."

"Do you love him?" I asked the question seriously, but it was really just for kicks.

"I did," she answered immediately and without regret, but there was something dead there.

We provided her with general tips, but it seemed Julia had already entertained the idea of most of them. Two of my coworkers helped explain the ground rules and another fed a line of paperwork, which she signed one right after another.

She was calm and emotionless, and I just kept thinking, *this is so great.* But I had to know why she was doing it. I was confounded, mesmerized even, so I waited until the completion of business and let the room grow still. "You don't have to say, and I really don't have to know...but I'm curious, Julia. Why are you doing this? What's changed?"

She hesitated but eventually gave in. "I'm married to the man that killed my first husband."

Oh, this was more perfect than I could have imagined. It was foolproof. Adrian De Luca would be my collar, and my secret weapon was his broken, pushed-too-far, vengeance-seeking wife.

"And you know this for a fact?" I asked.

"For a fact," she said flatly. "He may not have pulled the trigger, but his fingerprints are on the bullet. I'm sure you know how that works."

"I do. I certainly do."

TWENTY-FOUR

Adrian

THE FIRST HALF of the robbery was as seamless as our wedding. It went off without a hitch, which is more than I can say for the days and months that followed. I liked to live with a backup plan for my backup plan, and this time it really came in handy, because nothing after the grab, and I do mean nothing, went according to plan.

Roger was the best one-man show I'd ever had the pleasure of working with. He did almost all the heavy lifting, and performed each task exactly as he said he would. He delivered his routine security check at the Ainsley estate about a month prior to the robbery and, while he was there, installed software that would short not only the jewelry display wall locks but also the entire home security system for precisely two hours on the night of the robbery. This gave Holly plenty of time to enter the home and pop open the displays for a little cleaning. Once she was out, Roger erased evidence of the short with nothing more than a few keystrokes.

Charles Ainsley lived in a "smart home," but the question is, did he end up feeling that way? My guess was that he arrived home from Paris early Sunday morning and regretted more than one of his past choices, and toward the top of the list was sharing his vacation schedule with the help—not that he could link a single one of them to the robbery.

Holly's game was on point; her cousin Mickey, however, was not as brilliant, but this should not have come as a surprise to me. He and Dale had one job and one job only. Well, they actually had two jobs: First, they would drop Holly off on a side road that led to the woods behind the Ainsley estate. This would ensure none of the neighbors would be able to spot or describe a car when the police came around asking questions. While Holly was making her way through the wooded area and into the mansion, Dale and Mickey would take a drive until she came over the walkie-talkie to announce that she was on her way back to the car. But for some reason, probably because they're stupid and lazy, they sat in the drop-off spot and let the car idle until Holly's return.

When she radioed to tell them she was on her way back, they said, "Perfect, we'll be waiting," and they were; it's just that they couldn't drive away because the imbeciles were now out of gas. They apparently called Dominic, who undoubtedly ripped them a new one before explaining that he simply could not leave the wedding reception to bring them gas, because people were watching. So, like the wiseguy he was, Dom instead paid his newly licensed nephew, Tito, to deliver gas to our unfortunately ill-equipped business partners.

Meanwhile, a police car drove slowly by Mickey's car, and before it could turn around and circle back, Holly got out of the car and ran into the woods with the jewels. Thank God she did, because pretty soon the cops were back, and this time they had their lights going and they were up in the window asking questions. Thing One and Thing Two had to step out of the car and explain themselves, and who knows if the cops were believing their story or not, but in the nick of time, Tito showed up with the gas can and everyone was off the hook. The police left; Mickey's car was back in business; and Holly, on foot, had made it a mile down the road.

Dom called Tito and, when he heard how things were going, instructed him to find Holly and drive her home. Holly gift wrapped the jewels and passed them off to Tito, who then delivered them to the wedding. Dom intercepted the package, made eye contact with me as he placed it on the table, and it sat there all night without more than a handful of people knowing that $4 million worth of jewelry had joined the party. Dominic, pretending to pull best man duty, helped carry out the gifts and made sure the one with the jewels ended up in his car.

Julia and I had the house for the night, so we took advantage of the master suite and slept in the next morning. Despite how riled up I was over the score, I'd honestly never had a better night's sleep in my life. Everything had worked out: The robbery had gone off undetected; Dom was taking care of our business, while I made love to my new wife; and we were millionaires again—well, as soon as we made the sale. Julia and I spent the day after the wedding at the spa—hey, not the most masculine thing, but don't knock it until you try it—and it wasn't until the following Monday that I found out about Mickey's blunders in their entirety. Dominic, who hated Mickey even more than I did, was happy to share the news.

"Told you we never should have hired him. Things really could have gone south this time, Adrian."

"I know, I know. He's a schmuck, so what's new? But it all worked out, didn't it?"

"Yeah, thanks to frickin' Tito."

"We should really make a play for that kid. He's a natural."

"Yeah, yeah." Dom rolled his eyes. "My sister would kill me if she knew. She wants nothing to do with this, always saying 'I want a normal life for my babies!'" I laughed at Dominic's high-pitched lady voice.

"And yet, she was happy to show her face at the wedding."

"She's always had a thing for you."

"Really? Serafina? Hmm...and where was this information fifteen years ago?"

"Focus on the sale, would ya?"

Selling stolen goods, especially something as specific as the jewels, was always a tricky endeavor, but being in cahoots with the richest, greediest bastards you could ever imagine sure helped. In this situation, the best possible customer was one who valued discretion. They understood this purchase as one to admire, not one to flaunt, and truth be told, they may not even have wanted to.

Some people simply love spending time around rare and beautiful things, but this wasn't solely about owning shiny baubles. What really got our target buyers' rocks off was the narcissistic beauty of owning something that someone else can't have and, better yet, something that someone else *used* to have or *should* have. When it came to this particular score, they didn't need the world to know they got what they got; they were just satisfied to be the guy who won the privilege of tucking it into bed each night. Sick, yes, but I didn't judge, because I knew the thrill ride they were on, and even if I didn't, it wouldn't matter. I was happy to cash in on pretty much any opportunity, personality disorders included, as long as it didn't endanger children or put my crew at unnecessary risk.

A bit of networking led me to a buyer who was interested in purchasing the entire collection, which was music to my ears, and we had it all set up before the robbery even happened. I planned our entire honeymoon around the meeting with the buyer, not that Julia knew any of this.

She'd originally been in favor of doing the honeymoon immediately following the wedding, but I talked her into a few weeks of rest. Now that the time had come, we got on a private plane and I asked if she regretted the choice to postpone.

"No, I think it works out better this way," she said, and I had to agree.

Julia napped for the next few hours, and when she woke up, I said, "Welcome to Mexico."

"Mexico? What happened to the Cook Islands?"

"We're still going. I just needed to make a little pit stop."

"For what? Tequila?"

"Business, that's all. Don't worry about it," I laughed. Then I waited for the plane to taxi inside the hangar. With the hangar door now closed, I gave Julia a kiss on the forehead and hopped out of the plane. It felt good to stretch my legs but even better to see Alonzo Cortez, a high-ranking member of the Mexican cartel, standing before me with a full duffel bag. Alonzo was there to represent our buyer, his boss, Victor Hernandez—God strike me dead if there's not at least a thousand men living with that same name. "Good to see you." I stretched out my arm and shook

Alonzo's hand.

"Likewise. Listen Adrian, I have to be upfront with you. Victor ran into a temporary cash flow problem. I've only got half," he said, motioning toward the bag.

"I thought it looked a little small." I tried to keep it cool. "Does he still want the rest?"

"Definitely. Can pay in full in about a month."

"With interest?"

"Of course. Twenty percent, plus a little extra for your troubles."

"I can agree to that." My spirits were beginning to perk back up, and they skyrocketed when he opened the zipper. I don't care what anyone says, stacked money is an aphrodisiac. I withheld part of the merchandise, switching baggage and a few friendly gestures because I liked the guy. "Heard tell of a lot of crazy true stories, but never a time Victor being short on cash. What's going on down here?"

"Brother," he said with a heavy smile. "You wouldn't believe me if I told you."

"Give Victor my best," I chuckled and turned to leave. I opened the door to the plane and told Julia to grab her stuff. "Come on, we're switching."

She looked confused but did as she was told. I called Dom, and in a matter of hours, we touched down in Chicago where he was waiting, right on time as always.

"Would it be a huge score if everything went right?" He winked.

"I assume you know where to put these?" I asked.

"Hiding spot numero dos, I'm guessing."

"I see what you did there. I'm just not in the mood to laugh. But yes, the second spot on the list would be great."

Once again, Julia and I switched planes, but this time we were off to the Cook Islands for real. She was annoyed and not in a great mood, I could tell, so I went out of my way to force our first day in paradise to be ultra-romantic—or so I thought. It was difficult to focus on anything but getting that money deposited, which Julia brought up during our room service dinner.

"Can we please just do the bank thing tomorrow and get it out of the way?"

"Uh...yeah, sure. If that's what you want."

"What I want is to get out of this room and go enjoy ourselves, but that's kind of hard to do when we're sitting on a pile of money, isn't it?" she asked, proving she had more insight into my mind than I'd originally guessed.

"It sure is."

"And we're not getting room service tomorrow. Not even for breakfast."

"Julia, this is a five-star resort. The food is amazing."

She rolled her eyes and changed into boring pajamas.

"Why would you even bring those to a honeymoon?"

"You brought fake passports and are putting me to work, so I really don't think you have room to talk," she said, because she's always known how to put me in my place.

Fair enough, baby. Fair enough.

TWENTY-FIVE

Julia

ADRIAN QUIZZED ME all morning, and once he felt I could recite each piece of the new me—or at least what those fake documents said about a woman named Miriam Jacobs—backward and in my sleep, we set off for the bank. He thought it best if I went in alone, and I was happy to oblige. Had the Feds not known what I was up to, I'd have been a nervous wreck, but I drew confidence from picturing Adrian rotting in a prison cell.

As I sat waiting, I thought about those doctored documents and came to the conclusion that they were as real as anything else, because I had no idea who I was at this point. I was so many people all at one time, but the person I was the least was myself, and it hit me as being so ironic that I'd started out on this journey with Adrian because I thought he was helping me be me again. But all he'd really done was ruin me, and all I had left to do was make sure he came tumbling down as well.

The account was set up and the money safely deposited without a single snag, just as Adrian said it would. All that was left to do was wait while keeping up the act, so I forced myself to lighten up, to try and appear as in love as possible. It was, after all, our honeymoon, and Adrian would be suspicious if I kept acting strange. I thought I was doing a good job but shook like a leaf when he questioned my mood two days after the bank.

"Is something wrong? Are you still mad at me?" he asked.

"No."

"Are you sure? I promise I won't do business on another romantic trip ever again if that's what you want."

"Okay...good." I tried to act like he'd hit the nail on the head and reminded myself probably once an hour to up my game. When it turned my stomach, I assured myself the misery wouldn't last forever, that I would soon be free.

Adrian and I went jet skiing and snorkeling, but other than that, we spent most of our time relaxing at the beach or lounging by the pool and, of course, drinking. Alcohol became an applied science for me. With too much, I knew I would slip, but I needed just enough to keep the edge off. They call it liquid courage for a reason I now completely understand.

I tried to spot Agent Bradshaw and her coworkers, but it wasn't until our final evening that I recognized even one of them. Adrian and I had gone to dinner at an open-air bar and grille, and I saw Dan, one of the agents, when he stood from his place at the bar and dropped a few dollar bills into the live entertainment's tip jar.

For one dangerous moment, our eyes met. *Save me*, I begged.

Take me out of here—not out of the bar or off the island but out of this life of playing dress up. I thought they'd have come and gotten me by now. I thought that when I deposited that money, they'd have all they needed to make an arrest. But apparently they didn't, and I'd have to lie and suffer and fake my way through loving Adrian a little longer. The not knowing how long felt like being poisoned, and I wished I could go back to the night before the wedding and run the way Dominic suggested.

Why do we think we know better? All those sayings I'd heard urging a person to not make decisions when they're sad or angry, and what did I do? I made a decision when the only thing I was more than sad was angry. Why did I think I could do this?

Back in Chicago, Agent Bradshaw hammered me with questions. She was pissed I hadn't told her about Mexico, and I was pissed she didn't understand that I didn't know about it until we were there.

"When are you going to arrest him?"

"We don't have enough evidence yet."

"You know about the money, where it came from."

"Did you see the jewels, Julia? Did you witness the exchange?"

Both questions deserved a big fat no. Adrian hadn't even mentioned the jewels, let alone shown me, and he'd gone into a side room to make the exchange in Mexico, an office of sorts, from what I could peep. "Just get the evidence. I know he did it. I can't take this anymore."

"Then you'll have to get us more information." There was a threatening tone to it, and for a second, I think I hated her more than Adrian did. The good news was that I'd only deposited half of what the jewels were supposedly worth, and Agent Bradshaw and I both knew there had to be another sale happening. "Find out what he's doing next. You live with the man. It shouldn't be difficult."

There were a lot of things that "shouldn't be" but were indeed, and all I wanted to do was return to my old house. Living in Adrian's city loft was once a luxuriously romantic idea to me, but now it seemed a forced labor prison and I wanted out more than ever.

TWENTY-SIX

Dominic

DO YOU KNOW how difficult it is to keep a group of wiseguys calm after a big score? It's like herding cats, except in this case, the cats had bad decision-making skills and the catnip was a boatload of money. Thank God only a few of our guys knew about the jewelry heist, but the others largely suspected our involvement, and they wouldn't shut up about it.

The good thing about Dale and Mickey being seen by the cops that night was that it threw the authorities off our trail. Adrian and me had a few days to ourselves, and that was nice while it lasted, but we knew they'd be coming our way. It was, after all, Mickey Mouse they questioned first, and I can only imagine the stupidity that came oozing out of that interview. We'd advised him to lie low for a while. "Don't contact us, Mickey. It's just like when you give a girl your number and she's inevitably not interested: Don't call me; I'll call you." He may not have appreciated the joke, but he must have gotten the message, because there for the first week or so, he did as he was told.

The Feds showed up to Fancy's just like we figured, and we gave them nothing, same as always. Adrian burst out laughing when they asked if we knew Mickey. "Oh, come on, you think ole Santino did this?"

"We have reason to believe he was involved, yes."

"Ha! Well, let me know if he is, because if Mickey Santino pulled this off, I'm gonna start preparing for the apocalypse."

"What about you, Dominic?" Agent Bradshaw asked. "What do you know about Mr. Santino?"

"Well, I've known him since high school, but no one's ever had reason to call him Mr. Santino."

"So then you also know his cousin, Holly."

"Yeah. Nice girl."

"Are you aware of by whom she is employed?"

"You're gonna have to repeat that sentence in modern-day English," I said, playing dumb, but mostly I just wanted to bust her balls for trying to sound unnecessarily smart.

"Do you know where she works?" Bradshaw restated, clearly annoyed.

"She works parties and stuff, I think. Like a caterer or something."

"So neither of you are aware of her recent departure from Charles Ainsley's employ?"

Adrian and I looked at each other. No, we weren't aware, and that was the truth.

"Tell me, gentlemen, where would you hide four million

dollars' worth of stolen jewelry?"

"You're implying we have experience in that sort of thing," Adrian said, faking offense.

"Can you just play along?"

"Well sure. Let's say I'm the thief you're implying I am. Why would I give you ideas for places to look? That's like me coming into your office and asking how it is you get bugs into my places of legitimate business. If you think I had something to do with that robbery, prove it."

"Oh, I will."

"But not today. You've got nothing. Why else would you be here without warrant or arrest?"

"To get under your skin."

"Feel free to have a drink. It's on me." Adrian began to turn and leave, but Agent Bradshaw wasn't through.

"You never said where you'd hide the jewels, Adrian."

"If I had something as hot as that load of jewels...well, I'd find one hell of a hiding place and sit on it like a hen. And then I'd tell you to piss off and come back when you're smart enough to do your own job."

"You know, I think I'll stick around for that drink."

"Just don't stay too long, will ya? No offense, but you're not the type of woman my customers are here to see."

Leave it to Adrian to throw gasoline on an already blazing fire. "You know, you could have been a little cooler back there," I said to him later.

"That lady drives me up a wall. She's hunting us, Dom. It irks me."

"Me too, but all you're doing is making her want you more."

"I know. I can't help it."

I don't know if it was because of the fact that I knew his

personal life was about to implode or my blossoming sense of self-reliance, but something was causing me to see Adrian in a different light. He appeared more flawed than he had ever been in my eyes, and in a real way, I entertained the idea that maybe Adrian wasn't always the guy with all the answers. Maybe I was his right hand for a reason beyond brotherhood. Maybe I stood in a place of honor not given to me out of pity but because I'd earned it. Maybe I was the man I'd once almost been. Maybe I didn't need Adrian.

But still, I protected him, even from Julia. She came to me after the honeymoon, depressed and full of fear. "I need help," she said.

"I want to help you, but I won't play double agent."

"I need information, that's all. Just a little. Just something they could use to put him away."

"Julia..."

"You said you'd help!"

"I said I'd help *you*. Not the Feds."

"But you guys pulled the heist, right? It was definitely you?"

"Do you not understand that I've already gone too far? I'm a dead man walking."

"So am I."

"It didn't have to be this way. I offered you a way out."

"You offered me a temporary solution. I want something more permanent."

"What do you think this crew will do when they find out what we've done?"

"Hopefully they'll be behind bars."

"That doesn't stop business from rolling right along," I chuckled. "You'll run, Julia. It's only a matter of when." She cried, which made me feel miserable, but there was nothing I could do.

"Listen. When you want to run, I'll help you. But until then, do what you gotta do, and do it by yourself."

"Are you mad at me?"

"No."

"Then why are you being like this?"

"Being like what? If Adrian's going down, I'm going down with him. I'm guilty of everything he's guilty of. What am I supposed to do?"

"Well, I'm sorry I bothered you, Dom." She walked away, filling me with instantaneous regret.

TWENTY-SEVEN

Julia

I THOUGHT I'D reached the epitome of being let down, but my talk with Dominic sent me into a new low. I understood why he wasn't happy with me, and maybe I'd hurt his ego a bit. But I really thought he'd give me something, a pity morsel at least. Agent Bradshaw was on my back, and I wanted that information just as bad as she did, but I had my work cut out for me. I wish I could say that my acting skills saved the day, and I wish I could have loved the answers right out of Adrian, but both would be a lie. Things went another way for us.

I watched that man like a hawk, asked him a million questions every time he came in or went out. Holly Gadaldi called our house one night and I accused him of having an affair. The sick thing was that, for one second, I hoped it was true so that I could divorce him for legitimate reasons and, even though he said I was crazy, I would have pursued it had the idea of him cheating not made me so jealous.

I became a shrew, a complete and utter shrew, and it blindsided Adrian and me both. The thing that likely saved me was the fact that, as far as Adrian knew, his guys were married to shrews as well. Perhaps he used it as an opportunity to relate to his crew and join the conversation named "Listen to the latest ridiculousness my wife just pulled; just listen to what I'm dealing with—poor, pitiful mobster me."

I had never given him a reason to chime in before we were married, and doing so now found me honestly disappointed in myself. I hadn't been that way with Patrick, and I prided myself on that. I would've done the same with Adrian, had every intention of doing so, but that was before.

So what happened to us? I often wondered how Adrian would answer that question. Maybe he excused the change in our relationship as "what goes up must come down." That would have been the most logical explanation, but then again there never was much logic to Adrian and me. We didn't fit, and yet at one time I'd sworn we were made for each other. At the time, I'd accepted it with relief, maybe even a giggle. But now everything was different, and so was I.

Had I never known Adrian's link to Patrick, the bubble would have never been burst. We would have kept going up, up, up, and I'd have had no need to be terrible, and my many worries would have been but a reasonable few. I knew this because, even though I hated Adrian, even though I was planning his end, I mourned his exit from my life. I'd married him, but what I did that day was send him away. In the physical, he stood right before me, but from my heart, he was gone, and it left a hole larger than any loss I'd ever known, because it was cumulative.

He'd been ripped from my life, the life I thought we'd share, and left behind the roots of barren scars. Small shards of what I thought had healed remained, but at random, and it became clear to me that I had no control over them. I tried but couldn't mourn them the way I wanted to. I knew they were there, but they wouldn't listen. Why wouldn't they listen? Why couldn't Patrick hear me? Why would he not come to me? I used to have dreams about him, even after Adrian, but now he was gone, and I needed him.

I'd spent so many hours on *what if.* What if I'd planned spaghetti instead of lasagna? What if I'd remembered the ricotta cheese? What if Patrick had stayed at work longer or left earlier? What if I'd have complained about him stopping at the liquor store so often? He shouldn't have gone there all the time; it wasn't safe. I shouldn't have made lasagna, and Patrick shouldn't be dead, but *bad things happen to good people.* It became my mantra, and it got me through the day, but that was before the truth came and shut me right up. Adrian stole *what if* from me, the place I would go to remember that I almost lived in the world I used to love. I was so close—just one *what if* away—and for a while it was comfort enough.

But now *what if* was gone, and my truth was that it didn't matter what was for dinner the night Patrick died. It would never matter if he liked to stop at a run-down liquor store or a synagogue. There was no such thing as a perfect time to leave the office, because he would have died either way, and Adrian would have made it so.

He took everything from me. It's just that I didn't understand: If I was numb, how could it hurt so badly?

TWENTY-EIGHT

Adrian

WHY IS IT that when we're happy, we can't be completely happy? We're waiting for the other shoe to drop. Surely it won't stay like this forever, we think. Something bad will happen. But when things are actually bad, we forget about the other shoe. We think we'll be sad forever. We consider the idea of feeling or being better, and although we think it's possible, we just can't visualize our lives making the jump. How will this ever get better? When will it stop feeling this way, we ask.

That's how I felt those first few months of marriage. My Julia was still in there somewhere, but something unexplainable had happened. It had to be more than the nagging and complaining, but I couldn't say what it was. She and I fought all the time. I wanted to know why she wasn't affectionate anymore, why she avoided sex so often. She wanted to know why I worked all the time. I could handle the fights and anger, but it seemed she was disappointed more than anything, and that made me feel like such a failure. How could I have let her down? How could it have happened so quickly?

She was right. I worked too much, and even though the hours were actually no longer than I'd always kept, I was slipping. Before the robbery, I'd at least paid Julia the attention she deserved. Realizing it put to rest every preconceived notion I'd ever had about other people's marriages. No judgment here, no sir.

Our fights were somewhat of a broken record, but nothing that was said or done during these arguments ever fixed anything. It always led to Julia complaining. "I just want a normal life," she'd say, and for half a second, I wanted to give her one if she promised to cheer up. But then I'd just get upset.

"Normal. Ha! Julia, what is normal? What does that even mean? Is normal a good thing? I don't know, I think it's supposed to be. Are we supposed to want normal? If normal means waking up every day just to take another man's orders, then count me out."

"Tons of people take your orders."

"Yeah, and that's my point."

"You were them once."

"Not anytime recently."

"And you still take orders."

"Not very many, Julia."

"But you take them."

"What's your endgame here? Why are you being like this?"

"Being like what?"

"All this talk about normal. Like what you really want is your old boring life. No offense to Patrick, I'm sure he was a good guy. But I'm not him and my goals in life don't begin or end at a family vehicle with a five-star safety rating and a built-in GPS I don't need, because my steady-yet-meaningless job has me driving to the same stupid place every day. And you knew that before you married me, so don't act like you're doing me some kind of favor."

"And what? You saved me from a life of boring, is that it?"

"Somethin' like that, yeah."

"I didn't ask to be rescued."

"And I didn't ask for an interrogation. But here you are... questioning my life."

"If that's what I'm doing, I'm a little late, don't you think?"

I didn't know what to think. Our relationship was in shambles right out of the gate, but for some reason, she and I were holding on. Our marriage was working; it just wasn't what I thought it'd be. And now Julia was questioning everything about me. I brought home a mink and a diamond necklace one night, and she didn't even bat an eye.

"Why do you have to steal things?"

"So it fell off a truck, no big deal."

"No big deal? Adrian, these things don't belong to us."

"Julia, do you think these big companies care about you or me? Not for a second. They've got insurance out the crapper, and hell, sometimes they even set up the hit themselves. When people steal from them, they're basically making money."

"You mean when things fall off their truck."

"See, you're catching on."

"But why do you have to do it like this?"

"Don't act like we're the bad guys."

"Then what are you?"

"There's always gonna be bad guys. We're the filter."

"You could make money some other way."

"It's not always about the money. We do good things for people...I do good things for people."

"Like Robin Hood? You're a man in tights now?"

"Very funny, but no, not really, that's not how it is."

"Then how is it?"

"I think we're made who we are for a reason. I'm no angel, but I think sometimes God...well, maybe He doesn't always approve of my method, but there are times I think He's pretty pleased with the end result."

"So let me get this straight. You're looking me in the eye right now and saying you're on God's side."

"I'm saying I hope He's on mine."

"Do you think He is?"

"What I think is that He's real. We're supposed to act like Him, right? Well, I don't know if that's exactly what I do, but on certain days, I like to think so."

"Is it possible that you sometimes play for the other team?"

"You mean the devil?"

"Yes."

"The way I see it, there's God and there's the devil, and if there's a war going on between the two, well...I suppose we'd better know 'em both."

"Know yourself, know your enemy?"

"Exactly. The eleventh commandment."

The truth was, I didn't know exactly what God thought of me—still don't. But what I did know was that, when God made man, He did so with the gangster in mind. The proof is in the way we're wired. No one compartmentalizes more than the gangster. How else could I orchestrate a stolen jewelry deal with the Mexican cartel, all while running an entire family and trying to keep my marriage from one-hundred-percent implosion?

Victor got in touch and said he had the money. "I've got everything except interest." I appreciated that he told me ahead of time or else I'd have been especially ticked. Regardless, we made a new deal. He'd pay the other half of the $4 million, and I'd bring him everything except the dime piece of the entire collection: a hefty blue diamond ring worth three-quarters of a mill all on its own. I'd give him a chance to buy it outright, and that would serve as his interest payment.

He agreed to the deal, and to top it off, he agreed to meet in Chicago. We made the switch at three in the morning, and I went straight home to wake up Julia. It was time for her to fly to The Cooks again.

She wouldn't be happy, but I was. It was something I hadn't felt in several weeks, and it occurred to me how powerful joy can really be. Most people hunt happiness like it's something we have to earn, and in some ways maybe we do. Either way, joy does eventually come along. Maybe we deserve it; maybe we don't. But the universe thinks we do, and the universe doesn't play favorites—neither does the Mexican cartel. I don't think God plays favorites, and you know what, I bet Robin Hood didn't either.

TWENTY-NINE

Julia

"IT'S FOUR IN the morning," I groaned, covering my head with a pillow.

"I'm aware."

"Just let me sleep a few more hours." I was groggy and wanted the extra rest, but in another way I was wide awake and beginning to panic. Agent Bradshaw had wanted me to find out when the next sale was going down, but she didn't seem to understand that it was easier said than done. If it was so easy, why couldn't she do it? It was her job!

"Come on, Julia, this is for our future. Look, I brought coffee."

"I'm not packed."

"I'll help you," he said, pulling me into a seated position, and

179

it was then that I saw the duffel bag full of cash sitting by the bedroom door.

"You've got your own packing to do."

"No, I'm not going."

"What? I don't want to go by myself."

"You're not. Tami's going with for a nice girls' getaway."

"How will Two Guns survive without her cooking?"

"It's only four days. He'll figure it out." Adrian shrugged it off while rifling through my bathing suit drawer. "Here, take this one. It's my favorite. On second thought, leave it here."

"I can pack myself. It's fine."

"Okay, they'll be here in an hour."

"They?"

"Tony and Tami. The Feds are watching too close. I'm staying out of this one."

"Makes sense...," I said, fighting tears. How could this be happening again?

"Hey...hey, what's wrong, baby? It'll all work out just like last time. You're a pro."

"I just...I'm sorry, I just don't want to go without you."

"Julia, we can go again some other time. Just you and me, okay?"

I nodded along and pulled away when he tried to kiss me. He left me alone to pack, and by the time my ride arrived, I was ready to be Miriam Jacobs again, but this time Miriam had a plan of her own.

On the way to the airport, I "realized" out loud that the perfect beach dress was hanging in the closet at my old house and asked Two Guns if he would let me run inside. "It'll only take a minute. Come on, we're like two blocks away."

"We'll just buy another when we get there." *Tami and her*

bright ideas.

"We could but...okay guys, the truth is that Adrian gave me coffee on an empty stomach, and...I just really need a bathroom, okay?"

"Aye aye aye, good grief, Julia, just make it fast," Two Guns agreed as he turned down my old street. "We can't be late."

"Pop the trunk, will ya? I need my suitcase," I said as I got out of the back seat.

"For what? I thought you had to shit!"

"I do, but I still want that dress."

In place of the profanities he was likely thinking, Two Guns, who'd probably been up all night, released a heavy sigh and reached beside his seat to unlatch the trunk.

"I'll be fast!" I promised and ran inside with the suitcase. Before leaving the loft, I'd taken half the money from the duffel bag and stuffed the empty middle space with shoes, a set of bed sheets, and random articles of clothing. Now, I emptied $1 million worth of cash from my suitcase and shoved half the bills into the bottom of a used bag of dog food I had left over from a week of dog sitting. I washed the Puppy Chow residue off my hands and arms. Then I went upstairs to load the rest of the cash into the bottom of a box I used to store accessories from old workout equipment.

"Was I fast enough?" I asked Two Guns upon my return to the back seat.

"You did good," he assured, looking at the clock and then at me through the rearview mirror. I saw the corners of his eyes pull up into a smile and I returned the sentiment, wondering how bad *good* could be.

I once asked Adrian how it was that he paid for all the private plane rides, to which he answered, "I don't." Of course he didn't pay for them. There's not much Adrian actually paid for, and now that I think of it, I'm not even sure he was required to pay an electric bill—at home or at Fancy's or any of the random warehouses he owned, not that his name was on a single deed.

Tami and I flew to the Cook Islands courtesy of Miller Farrington, a pilot, businessman, and owner of a small regional airport that Adrian's crew happened to provide "security" for. The weather was perfect, so Tami went to the pool while I freshened up. The bodyguard Adrian hired to drive us from the airport to the hotel also accompanied me to the bank. I asked if I could have a copy of my last transaction and, once back at the hotel, snapped a picture of the deposit amount and texted it to Adrian, using our prepaid GoPhones, of course.

He replied—*great job, baby!!!!!!!!!!*—and made me promise to delete the picture I'd taken and shred the paper trail. I did as he said, and not five minutes later, my phone buzzed again. It was a text from Agent Bradshaw, whose number I'd entered as Bethany—because I knew two of them and they were both dating guys from the crew. *Hey Julia, haven't seen you around, wanna grab lunch?*

Wish I could, but Tami and I are living the island life.

Island life?

Yes, the boys surprised us spur of the moment.

Lucky you, she wrote, adding an emoji. What does it mean when a federal agent sends you a frowny face? Before I could decide, she sent another: *Business trip?*

A little but already done. Time to relax.

I see.

Rain check on lunch? See you in four days!

Yes! See you soon.

Okay, well she wasn't happy, but there was nothing I could do except have a ball with Tami on a trip that ended up feeling much too short. I dreaded returning to Chicago to face Agent Bradshaw and whatever plans she had for me next. In my wildest dreams, I hoped that she caught Adrian doing something incriminating while I was gone, but no such luck.

"Okay, so you deposited a million. That means there's still jewelry to be sold."

"You're not even going to ask about my trip?"

"Your tan is lovely, Julia. Let's focus." Agent Bradshaw went on to emphasize how important it was that I find out what was left of the collection and when he planned to sell it. "And if you could find out who the buyer is, even just a first name or anything, that'd be great."

"Yeah, and so would a billion dollars or an overnight cure for cancer, but I don't think either of those are immediately accessible."

"Do you not want this anymore? Or are you playing for Adrian's team again?"

"Are you kidding me? I want him caught just as badly as you do, but you've got to understand, the man will barely even tell me what he had for breakfast."

"I know this is hard, Julia, but we're running out of time. We either catch him or you're stuck with him, so figure something out."

Already did, I thought, smiling inside, but I put on a sour face.

After the meeting, I went to Fancy's with food from Adrian's favorite restaurant. Pleasantly surprised, Adrian took the food and kissed me but was soon called away to his office. "Sorry babe,

I gotta take this call," he said, leaving the half-eaten meal on the bar. Dominic and I were left behind to small talk, but as soon as Adrian was out of sight, I grabbed a pen from my purse and wrote *bugs?* on a cocktail napkin?

"I just did a sweep. We're clear."

"Good. You still got that stuff?"

"Be more specific."

"The documents."

"Which ones?"

"All of them," I said, referring to the passport, social security card, credit cards, and birth certificate—everything I'd need to run away.

"Why do you need them?"

"For a rainy day."

"You expecting a storm?"

"Just freaked out...feeling trapped. I wouldn't leave without telling you," I whispered.

"That's not all I'm worried about."

"Listen, help me or don't, but you said you would."

"Fine, I'll send 'em your way," he promised and made good on it three days later.

I was home alone when the doorbell rang, and I answered it to find a man holding a garment bag. "Julia De Luca?" I nodded a confirmation. "Delivery."

Delivery? I didn't order anything, and Adrian had pretty much given up buying me clothes, since I rarely ever liked his choices.

"Sign here." There was something off about this man, and as I signed, I tried to figure out what it was. He was dark-haired and wore sunglasses under his ball cap, but as he handed me the garment bag, he said, "Be good, Julia." As he turned to leave, everything clicked.

"You should stay blond."

"I think I will," Dominic said, descending the front steps, and after a few paces down the sidewalk, he raised his arm in a casual wave. "Have a nice day, ma'am," he said without looking back.

Once inside, I unzipped the bag and laughed when I found a nineties-inspired windbreaker running suit attached to the hanger. I'd always liked Dominic's sense of humor, but what I liked even better were the documents he'd slid into the inside pocket. It was a place normally meant for accessories, but what it held in this instance was my lifeline to a new existence, one Dominic apparently thought I should live as Savannah Frazier.

Within a week, the documents were buried in the backyard alongside the money I'd stashed away. I'd snuck over to the old house, wishing I didn't have to use the shovel, but I had a pretty good hiding place in mind. In early spring, I'd used an old tarp to protect susceptible flowers from the frost. Adrian and I became engaged soon after, and not once had I even thought about going out back to tend my mediocre garden.

I dug the hole and thought about my mother for the first real time in quite a while. She'd probably say I was digging the hole wrong or that I needed a new shovel, and both were likely so. My father's voice came to me: *There's more than one way to skin a cat, my love.* I wondered if he could see me, if he was trying to tell me to go another way.

I didn't know which way to go, which city I'd call home, but time was running out and I knew I needed to decide right away.

THIRTY

Julia

SOMETHING ABOUT OUR marriage was improving, but that didn't mean it wasn't still the pits. My guess is that Adrian and I were so honest about what we thought of each other that we no longer felt bad about most of what had transpired. It took the pressure off, or at least some of it, and we both just kept doing our own thing, loosely tethered to one another.

Getting information from Adrian was a continuously fruitless effort, but that didn't mean I'd stopped trying. Holly Gadaldi had called the house three times in a week. I knew she used to work as a maid at the Ainsley estate, and I figured she was involved in the heist, so I questioned it.

"Why does Holly keep calling here?"

"I told you, there's nothing going on between us."

"Then why does she call?"

"She asks business advice."

"Why would a maid need business advice?"

"I'm sorry, when did you become a prosecutor and why am I on trial?"

"Just answer the question."

"She's going to hair school or whatnot. Wants to open her own salon here in a few months."

With robbery money, I'm sure. "And what do you know about running a salon?"

"Why you got a problem with this?"

"I don't. I'm just curious."

"Didn't you ever hear that story about curiosity?"

I looked at him blankly.

"It killed the cat," he said and walked out.

A few days later, I came home and was surprised to see Mrs. Witherby, our elderly upstairs neighbor, sitting in the living room. "Mrs. Witherby...hi, how are you?"

"Oh, I've been better," she said, looking up from her needlepoint.

Just then Adrian came down the hallway and explained that Mrs. Witherby was staying for dinner.

"But like I told him, you can call me Florence," she said.

"I'll try to remember that." I smiled and followed Adrian down the hallway as I called out, "Hope you like eggplant parmesan."

"Love it!"

"Listen," Adrian said. "Some wannabe thugs have been stopping by Mrs. Witherby's place asking for her medication. It's become a regular thing and they're supposed to stop by again tonight."

"So what are you going to do about it?"

"Answer the door, scare them away, that's all."

"Right...I'm sure that's all," I said, rolling my eyes.

The three of us had a lovely meal, after which Adrian left us gals alone to watch *Jeopardy* and discuss Florence's wide feet. "I have to order my shoes from a catalog. It's so unhandy."

Somewhere in the middle of Double Jeopardy, we heard two loud thuds overhead, and when Adrian didn't answer his phone, I went looking for him, handgun in tow, of course. Mrs. Witherby's door was cracked open a hair and I peeked through, only to see Adrian crouched over two bodies.

"You freaking pre-laid the plastic?" I asked as he began to roll one of the perpetrators.

"Always be prepared."

"Did you learn that in Boy Scouts?"

"No. I was in it for two weeks but then my mother got in a fight with the den leader and never let me go back."

"That explains a lot."

"Yeah, yeah...go back to Mrs. Witherby, would ya? And don't tell her about this. I'll be down in a little bit."

Back in the living room, Mrs. Witherby asked if I figured out what the noise was and I made up a story about Adrian falling. "He's always had terrible balance."

"Did he trip over the ottoman? Because that darn thing is always in the way."

"You know, now that you mention it, I think it was the ottoman."

"Oh goodness, I think I'll get rid of it," she declared, and I promised I'd help her shop for a replacement. Thanks to Adrian and his preparedness, we wouldn't have to add area rugs to the list. He came home and assured Mrs. Witherby that the young men wouldn't be back to bother her.

"Are you sure?" she asked, seeming afraid.

"I'm sure."

"Well how'd you manage that?"

"We talked it out. Worked out a better plan."

"Well, wonderful. Walk me home. I'm tired."

When Adrian returned, I looked at him and smiled. "You talked it out?"

"A gun makes for a fine conversationalist," he grinned, and it made me laugh.

"Did you even try to hear them out?"

"No. And I know you're gonna ask why, so here it is: You just reach a point where you're tired of hearing people's shit. Once you're sure what they're all about, you just get it over with. I've got better things to do."

"Fair enough," I said but found it difficult to sleep that night, because I couldn't stop thinking about Adrian and the fact that it was impossible for me to stop falling for him. I thought about how patient he'd been with me the past few months without even knowing why I was being so terrible to him. My thoughts raced to Patrick's last day on earth and I wondered how much Adrian could even say about it.

I talked myself in and out of loving him the entire night long but eventually settled on out.

It's the charisma, I told myself. He was a conman; that's what he did—he conned his way through life. He was a professional liar who knew exactly what to say, when to say it, and when to stop saying it to keep me wanting more. There was truth in that, but the question of why always hung me up. Why? Why would he con me? He'd already won me, or so he thought. He wasn't trying to pull one over on me. He was trying to love me—like he'd promised. I was the one with a hammer in my hand, tiptoeing around the shards of a broken promise. I was the one deceiving. I was the one giving just enough to tease and never enough to satisfy, and even though there was burning hatred there, I felt so, so guilty.

I masked the guilt with the thought of what he would do to me when he put the pieces together, and it would happen soon. Like he said himself, he wouldn't have reason to hear me out: *Once you're sure what they're all about, you just get it over with.* In a few days, he and Two Guns would leave for a weekend business trip to New York, and when they left, so would I, except I wasn't coming back.

THIRTY-ONE

Julia

ADRIAN WAS PACKING a bag when my regular cell phone rang. It was my mother, so I let it go to voicemail. I thought Adrian would have left for New York already, and I was waiting on him to be gone so that I could pack my things and make a break for it. I got bored waiting for him to get out of my hair, so I played Helen's message:

Hi Julia, it's your mother. Is your new husband around? I'd love to speak to him, tell him what a slut he got hold of. Honestly Julia, it hasn't even been a year! You should be ashamed, and I'm telling you, I certainly was when I got the call. Seems your Aunt Irene stumbled upon your picture on the internet, some gossip site or something. Do you remember your Aunt Irene or have you abandoned her as well? Did you think no one would find out, or were you planning to just keep on lying? Your father is rolling over in his grave, I'm sure!

Burning-hot tears I couldn't wipe away soon enough raced down my cheeks.

Adrian walked in and came to my side. "What's wrong?" I replayed the message and thought he was going to shoot through the ceiling. "Julia, you need to nip this in the bud. This has gone on for too long."

"But she's my mother. What am I supposed to do?"

"You tell her she's not going to treat you like this."

"Like what, the person that she is? She's not going to change. She's always been like this."

"Then cut her off. Get rid of her."

"Adrian..."

"I only mean stop taking her calls, don't play her messages. Change your number if you have to. I've been begging you to get rid of that phone for months anyway."

"It's fine. I'll be fine. She just caught me off guard."

"Well are you going to call her back?"

"Not right away. I don't want to think about it right now."

"Okay, well when you do, you wear your black suit."

"What does that mean?"

"It means you're not taking her crap."

"So what does a black suit have to do with it?"

"It's an old tradition my dad started. It was a way to send a message without having to say a single word. If he was pinched, there would eventually be a court date and sometimes that court date was how he communicated with his guys, or the judge, or some participant sitting in the crowd watching. Blue suit meant *I forgive you or let's work together.* It was a sign of hope...that things were going well. Black suit meant *you're dead to me, I hate you.* In the right circumstance, the black suit told his guys he was putting out a hit. It was a 'this means war' kind of thing."

"Interesting."

"Yeah, kind of cool."

"But I don't want to go to war with my mother." At first he didn't respond, and I could tell there was something he wasn't saying. "What?"

"Well...I don't want to make you feel any worse, but...haven't you been at war with her this whole time?"

"No."

"If not war with her, then war with yourself, I'd say." He kissed me on the forehead and headed toward the door. "See you in a couple days," he said, gathering his things in the entryway.

"Wait!" I said, following his path. He turned to face me and, for a moment, we just stared at each other. "I want to tell you good-bye," I said, kissing him on the lips.

THIRTY-TWO

Valentina

DOMINIC WAS ALWAYS special, and that may not mean much coming from me, but it was true and ran deeper than the fact that he was the baby of the family and my only son.

He had this awareness, a sincere thoughtfulness for others—a trait his father mostly lacked. Being married to a mob man is of course a hard life full of hard people, hard times, and hard places to lay your head, but it was the life I'd led, and all things considered, it treated me fairly well. I couldn't complain, but I could write a book. It's just that most people wouldn't even believe the table of contents.

Rico was working for my father when we met, so it was difficult to get things off the ground. He asked permission to take me out but was turned down in a swift way. He tried again several times, but Daddy just kept saying no, so Rico and me started sneaking around. It was fun and exciting, like it is with most of these guys in the beginning, and maybe it was the fear of getting caught that really made it exhilarating. I just knew Daddy would catch us, but he didn't. Dead men aren't very observant.

I'd only been dating Rico a month when my father died in cold blood. I was twenty-one years old at the time and of course devastated. "I can't be with you anymore," I sobbed. "He didn't want this."

But Rico wouldn't give up and eventually convinced me that time would have seen my father come around. "You're his favorite. He liked me. He just wasn't ready for you to be serious with anyone, okay?" God only knows how much of that was true.

We were engaged and married, lickety-split. Serafina and Sophia were born fourteen months later and, I swear to you, Rico was begging for a boy before the twins could even sit up on their own. I made him wait a little longer, but we did have that boy, and thank Jesus himself, because Rico would have made me keep going until he got a son. Three children under the age of two didn't exactly suit my lifestyle, and it was my lifestyle that eventually landed me on kidney dialysis, not to mention my spotty lungs.

When Dominic visited during my treatments he usually sat quietly and listened to me babble on. There was a peaceful, confident way he carried himself, part of which was learned, but he did it better than everyone I knew, because the other part he was born with. This last time was different though. There were rushing waters below the surface of his glassy exterior, and it had little to do with the fact that my cough had grown nearly unstoppable and my voice raspier by the day.

"What is it, baby?" I asked.

"What? What is what?"

"There's something you're not saying. So say it."

"It's...complicated."

"Oh, honey, I have a PhD in complicated." I grinned. "Try me."

"Always talking about these degrees like they're real."

"School o' Hard Knocks is about as real as it gets. So spill it."

"Mom...this isn't about you...I don't want to talk about it."

"Okay fine, be that way. But I won't be around much longer, so if you want my feedback..."

He rolled his eyes and sat back in the chair, seeming to already regret what he was about to say but, at the same time, I could sense a curiosity in search of satisfaction.

"Why did Dad...Mom, why did he pick Adrian?"

Yup. There it was. Finally. "All this time and you ask now? I thought you'd come to terms."

"I have."

"But it bothers you."

"There are days."

"And others?"

"I figure I'm livin' a little thing called fate, or maybe it's destiny, I don't know. Doesn't matter."

"Mm-hmm..." I trailed off, my mind going back to the years when Dominic was a tiny thing. He and Rico were adorable together. My husband doted on the girls, but it was very clear that Dominic was his pride and joy. They were basically inseparable and it seemed to me, and really anyone with a brain, that Rico was grooming our son to take his place when the time came. So imagine my surprise when he came home one night and sighed, afraid to tell me, "We picked Adrian."

I sat up in bed, turned on the lamp, and said, "What do you

mean, *we* picked Adrian?"

"You know exactly what it means." He was right, I knew. I knew everyone loved both boys, but my husband had pull, and most people might think he'd have used that pull in favor of his son, but no, he recommended Adrian and everyone went along.

"Why do you favor him so?"

"It's not like that, Valentina..." He was trying to bite his tongue, but of course I gave him down the road about screwing over his own son, and I took him on the guilt trip of his life until finally he got up from the mattress, paced around to my side of the bed, and yanked the lamp out of the wall. He hurled it across the room, letting the sound of a shattering light bulb serve as the official end to our conversation.

"Mom?" The sound of Dominic's voice brought me back to the present.

"Yeah, yeah...I was just...you know, Dominic, the answer to your question is simple and complex at the same time."

"Try me," he winked, mimicking my earlier comment, one he'd heard from my lips at least a hundred times.

"Aren't you smart?" I half-smiled, coughing. "Your father loved what he did. Lived and breathed it, you know that. And he was tough. Tough on you kids and tough on his guys. He could be hard on me too, but we survived. Our life was so glamorous... until it wasn't. But then it would be glamorous again...and then someone would be murdered and another would go away, and things were always changing like that. I spent my life waiting for the other shoe to drop, and even though I liked the things and having fun with my girls...I was always bracing myself.

"Anyway, I never seen him scared o' nobody. Neither did you, if I had to guess...but you know, Dom, what you see isn't always the whole story. There were many nights he came home and I wondered if anyone in the world had ever looked so heavy. Just 'cause he wasn't scared doesn't mean he wasn't worried...and he couldn't hide that from me. He wouldn't talk about it, but I knew it. We fought about Adrian. I loved that boy, still do, but your father didn't budge when it came to him. He'd say, 'mind your own business, woman!'"

I had a good chuckle, a good round of coughing, and then I went on.

"The closest he ever came to explaining it was a half-clue I didn't understand at the time. He said, 'Heavy is the crown, Tina,' and of course I started an argument by correcting him: It's heavy *lies* the crown, moron!" Dominic seemed amused. "God, he was such a bull. But he had a heart too. He loved you. And he loved his life, but he wanted you to have something different. He wanted you to have a chance at being old," I said, a tear in my eye. "Took me a while to figure that one out. Cigarettes and booze were one thing, but it was the stress that killed him, baby."

"Then why didn't he say something?"

"What was he supposed to say? He couldn't exactly tell you not to do the thing he'd trained you to do, the thing he'd engrained into the lives of so many guys, Dom. How would that look? He was open to you doing something else, and had you done it, he would've given you hell for it. He would have run you through the mud at work but, deep down, he would've been happy. Relieved even. But when you stayed, he was still happy. He got his way, sorta. You were carrying on the family thing and doing the job in a way that made him proud, but he made it so it would take you longer to get to the throne, if at all, and that's what he wanted."

"That makes no sense."

"This life ain't about sense, Dominic, you know that. If we had more sense, we wouldn't be the people we are. If I had more sense,

I wouldn't be hooked up to this machine," I said, showing him the IV line.

A nurse walked in and removed the needle. "You're all done, Mrs. Abbatelli."

"Do you ever get tired of unpainted fingernails?" I asked her.

"We're not allowed to paint them. Hospital policy."

"That's not what I asked. I just wondered if you get tired of it. Not allowed to paint your nails? What is this, prison? A dictatorship? Do they pay you well enough to have boring nails?" I got a kick out of the bewilderment on her sweet little face.

"You'll have to excuse my mother," Dominic interjected, grabbing me by the arm. "She gets bored and loses her mind."

He took me to lunch and dropped me back home.

"What are you doing tonight?" I asked.

"Nothing."

"Lies." He kissed my cheek and grinned on his way out the door. It was the last time I ever saw him.

THIRTY-THREE

Julia

TAMI CALLED JUST two hours after Adrian left for
New York. "Oh, Julia, I'm so bored already."

"Already? Come on."

She asked what I was doing and I lied, told her I was having a
quiet night in and was thinking about running a bath. "Or maybe
a movie, I'm not sure."

"Mind if I join? I'm feeling so restless today."

"Tami, I—"

"I'll bring snacks! Wine, whatever you want."

"Sure," I relented. "It'll be fun."

"Oh, good! I'll be over in just a bit."

Tami had never struck me as the clingy type, and she and Two

Guns had been married for quite a while, so it seemed strange to me that she was having a hard time with him being gone for only a few days. The longer I thought about it, the more paranoid I became, so paranoid that I not only hid the suitcase I'd been packing, but I also put every single article back in the drawer it originally came from. I worried that Adrian was on to me and had sent Tami in as a deterrent, but when she came over, I was able to dismiss my suspicious thoughts.

We talked about how the guys had been working overtime lately, which seemed to be the reasoning behind Tami's sudden need for attention. Halfway through the movie—not that we were watching it—she brought up Dominic.

"Did you know he was originally supposed to go on this trip?"

"I guess I didn't."

"Yeah, Adrian called about a week ago and asked Tony if he could go in Dominic's place. It's a shame about his mother. She's really getting bad."

"Yeah, it's a sad thing. I understand why he wouldn't want to leave her for long periods of time."

"Me too. Poor Dom..."

"But she's still doing the treatments, right?"

"Yes. Crazy thing needs a kidney but I just don't think she's strong enough for a transplant."

"Very sad."

"Yup. But that's what happens when you smoke and drink your life away."

"Back in the day though, right?"

"Oh yeah, she's settled down quite a bit, but I'm a little older than you and I've known Valentina a long time. She and Rico lived life pretty wild. Those kids were the only thing that ever slowed 'em down, but not by much."

"Yeah, I've heard some stories."

"Well, I don't know which ones you've heard, but I guarantee every single one is true. Anyway, those twins are something else, still are."

"Whatever happened to them? Dominic doesn't talk about his sisters much."

"Oh no, he wouldn't. The girls both hated their father and got the hell outta dodge as soon as they could. It was a big scandal for a while and no one was supposed to talk about it. But after Rico passed, Tina mended fences. Apparently she told the girls, 'When you get to heaven, just act like we're still mad at each other. Your father will kill me.'"

For some reason, it struck me funny.

"But it didn't really amount to a whole lot. The girls have stayed gone and don't come around much. It's a wonder Dominic came out the way he did. Used to baffle me, and then one day I realized he's so calm because the poor kid never had a chance to talk growing up!"

"Could be."

"Well, enough of that. You know what we should do?"

"What?" I was almost afraid to ask.

"A Broadway play! I haven't been in forever. Let's go tomorrow night."

"I don't think I can, but I'd love to go some other time."

"Oh, you don't have plans. Let's go."

"I do have plans. Plans to go to bed early and sleep for as long as possible."

"Forget that, Julia, what are you, ninety?"

"Tami...," I complained.

"Well, I'm picking you up at two. We'll go shopping and get

dinner before."

"Okay, two o'clock," I agreed, knowing there was a chance she'd ring the doorbell and no one would be there to answer. It was what I wanted to do, but I lay in bed that night knowing how asinine it would be. If I wasn't there, she'd call her husband or mine, and not even a half-day's head start would be enough to escape the search party that would ensue.

So I slept in, had a relaxing afternoon, and answered the door to a still bubbly Tami. We had a nice evening despite the fact that I was constantly calculating how much time I had left until Adrian's return to Chicago. He was due back late Sunday evening. If I left early Sunday morning, it might be enough time, especially if I could talk Dominic into stalling Adrian somehow, which reminded me that I'd promised to give him a heads up.

Soon, I texted. Then I stared at the ceiling until I heard a knock on the door.

"How soon are we talking?" Dominic asked when I let him in.

"Will you invite Adrian for drinks when he gets back in town tomorrow night?"

"That's your big plan? Julia, we don't 'do drinks.'"

"I need you to stall him, that's all."

"I don't want to."

"He won't pin this on you."

"It's not that..."

"Then what's the problem?"

"I don't want you to leave."

"You'll know how to find me."

"Do you want me to find you?"

"Savannah would." I smiled and invited him to stay for a little while.

"Wish I could," he said. "But I've got some things to do."

"It's midnight."

"Like I said...got some things to do."

When neither of us could come up with something to say, he leaned in and kissed my cheek, and then he left without a word.

I stayed up for a while, mulling over my plan, which was to drive all day and night, maybe stop in a no-place town in western Iowa if I needed to rest. On Monday morning, I'd ditch my car, buy a new one, and head for Wyoming. I didn't know if I'd stay in the mountains or look up a childhood friend, but both seemed like viable options at the time. It felt like I was really doing this, like I could really get away from it all.

But I woke up the following morning to a phone call that more than wrinkled my escape plan.

THIRTY-FOUR

Adrian

RARELY DID I go back to New York, but when I did, it wasn't something I particularly enjoyed—too many ghosts. It's not that I was afraid of them; I just didn't like the inconvenience. But sometimes business required the trip, and this one in particular had offered the harvest we'd hoped for.

I was looking forward to being back in the Chicago city limits, but what I anticipated most eagerly was returning to Julia after she'd sent me away with a kiss. It wasn't a big deal in the grand scheme of things, but it had been a while since she'd made the effort, especially on the lips, and that excited me. I thought there was a chance she'd be waiting up for me, looking nice and interested in welcoming me home. But none of that happened.

I found her in a heap on the bedroom floor, hunched over a half-packed suitcase. She had raw, swollen eyes, and when she looked up, I swear to God, I thought she was leaving me.

"It was you, wasn't it?!" she screamed, and in that moment, I saw a side of Julia I'd never seen. It was an unraveling of something she'd kept hidden from me, and it gave me pause, took my thoughts to a place Julia had never given reason for me to go, but now there was an otherness to her, an animalistic rage I'd never dreamed she carried.

For a split second, I heard a voice saying, *she's not who you think she is,* but I settled on logic.

"What? What was me, baby?" I asked, taking a careful step toward her.

She stood to her feet and sort of laughed, "Don't play dumb with me."

"Julia. I have no idea what you're talking about."

She just stared at me, slowly shaking her head back and forth, seeming to wait on a confession to a crime I couldn't name.

"Absolutely no idea, Julia. Talk to me."

"Talk to you. Talk to you? About my dead mother? You want to talk about my dead mother?!"

"Your...baby, I'm sorry, I didn't know, I just didn't know..." I tried to move closer and take her in my arms, but she turned away and walked to the far side of the bed.

"How was New York?"

"Good. But I don't think that's what we need to discuss right now."

"Have you ever noticed how close New York is to Connecticut? You can get there in practically no time."

"Don't do this...don't go to that place."

"A person visiting New York for a few days would have more

than enough time to kill in Connecticut, plenty of time to set it up as a heart attack."

God knows I'd given Julia enough reasons to pin this one on me, and it made perfect sense. She'd seen my temper and my distaste for her mother. She knew I was capable of doing the thing she assumed, and it normally wouldn't bother me that a person thought I did something I didn't do. But this time, it tore me up.

"So how'd you do it?" she asked, climbing up on the bed, walking toward me on her knees. "Was it poison? Or did you go to shoot her and she just croaked before you could pull the trigger? Why was she in her garden, Adrian?! Did you march her out back, make her turn around?"

I took a step toward her and gently placed my hands around her upper arms. "I didn't do it, Julia. Swear to God."

"Why should I believe you?" She was crying, calmer now.

"Because I'm standing here telling you the truth."

"I can't believe anything you say!" she shouted. "You killed my..." She trailed off and began to sob, and it seemed like she wanted to go on but couldn't breathe.

"Julia...I didn't do it. I'm here. I'm so sorry...really, but I didn't do it...I'm here." I wanted to comfort her but felt like I was failing, probably because of the conflicted pain she must have been feeling. I guided her to the mattress and wrapped my arms around her. She fell into me, decades' worth of hurt tumbling out of her precious heart.

I didn't kill that lady, but sitting there listening to Julia like that made me wish I could. *Be glad you're already dead, Helen.*

THIRTY-FIVE

Julia

ADRIAN'S PHONE RANG, and my stomach did a dance as I remembered Dominic's promise to stall. It was Dominic on the line, but something seemed off when I heard Adrian say, "What? Just now? You're kidding. Man, I'm sorry. I'll be right over."

"His mom?"

"Yeah. She's gone."

"What a day."

"You're tellin' me. I don't want to leave you, but I need to go over there."

"You know what, I'll go with you."

"You sure?"

"Yeah, I need to get out and put my mind on something else. Be there for Dom."

"He would understand if you stayed home."

I knew he would, but I went anyway, and on the drive over, I told Adrian he didn't need to go to Connecticut with me. "I can handle it. You should stay here with Dominic."

"My place is with you, and Dom understands that. I'd tell him to do the same thing if the situation were reversed."

"You've known him longer. Valentina is practically your second mother."

"And she would tell me to go with you. The woman doesn't even want a funeral. She's always told us to throw her a party instead."

I'd grown a bit nervous by the time we reached the Abbatelli's, and Dominic looked surprised when he saw me. "It's good to see you," he said with a squeeze at the end of our hug.

"I'm really sorry about your mom," I said, and Adrian and I waited a while before we told him about my own.

We went home to pack for our Monday morning flight to Connecticut, but this time we flew commercial, and for those few hours, I felt some kind of normal again. Funny how death can bring you back to life.

Mrs. Shirley was delighted to meet Adrian, and he, like always, charmed her pants off—figuratively, of course. She helped us prepare the church, which took some time because, unlike Valentina Abbatelli, my mother had her funeral planned out from start to finish. There was even a piece of paper in her Bible that listed suggestions of things people could say about her.

"Who leaves funeral instructions in their Bible?" I asked.

"Well, I have a note in mine," Mrs. Shirley admitted.

Adrian wanted to know what it said.

"It says, *No Psalm 23 for me!*"

"That's it?" I laughed.

"That's all she wrote." Mrs. Shirley shooed the air and sort of laughed.

"What do you have against Psalm 23? Overused?"

"Tremendously so. And you know what else? Why is it such a sad passage? It's supposed to be encouraging, but it makes me feel blue. Plus, 'He makes me lie down in green pastures'? Sounds like something the Europeans do. I've never in my life lain down in a pasture, green or otherwise. Only two things you're gonna find there...cow patties and chiggers! The Lord made 'em both, but if you ask me, David got it wrong that time."

We chuckled at her ramblings, but she seemed unaffected and began straightening the hymnals on the back of each pew.

"That's a little excessive, don't you think?" Adrian was in disbelief.

"We've got to get this right. Because I'm telling you what... that woman will haunt us if we don't!"

Mrs. Shirley kept things lighthearted, but it wasn't enough, because there was nothing light about me. It's ironic, isn't it, that emptiness is so heavy?

"Well...it's over," Adrian said on our way home from the funeral. I nodded along but couldn't actually agree. It didn't feel over, and in truth, it wasn't. The burial had been postponed due to the frozen ground of an especially cold November.

Back at my parents' house, I asked Adrian if he wanted a cup of hot tea.

"Only if you're having one."

There was something happy about making the tea, but I sat at the table getting more and more sad. I snatched the napkins from the holder and stood for a moment before tossing them in the air. They floated down all around me and touched the floor like the last pebble of sand through an hourglass.

"Why are you crying?"

My mother was complicated but the answer to Adrian's question was not. "I thought she would change."

She'd given me no reason to believe this, but I thought one day I'd hang up the phone and feel something different. I waited for the day I could come home and feel warm. But even with her gone, there was a dampness that didn't require explanation, because the house that Helen built had always been made of stone.

We got in bed, but neither of us fell asleep right away. "Why is it that you thought she would change?" Adrian asked.

"I don't know, genetics maybe. Probably nature. No one wants a parent like that. We're wired to hope for something different."

"But you didn't get it."

"Not with her, no."

"Do you hate her for it?"

"Do you think I should?"

"Hard to hate a person who hates themselves so much already."

"Correct." I said it sadly and lay there listening to nothing until the heating vent rattled into duty.

"What about your dad?"

"I don't hate my father."

"No, I mean, did he think she would change?"

"I've thought about it before, and I don't know the answer, but I think maybe he did at first, when I was young. But then I think he just accepted what was."

"What makes you think that?"

I told him a story about my mother and how she didn't like it when my dad and I would have our own conversations or do anything without her. One time I mentioned a note he'd slipped into my lunchbox and she flipped. She didn't say anything, but I could tell she was upset. She double-checked my lunch on the way out the door every day for a month until she found what she was looking for. She yanked the note out and slid it into the back pocket of her slacks. Later that night, after dinner, I overheard her ask my father why he didn't leave notes for her.

"I guess I just don't have time in the mornings."

"You have time for Julia but not for me? Richard, you even drew a picture." I imagined she held up the note as Exhibit A.

"Helen, she's ten and a half years old."

"And you obviously love her more." She said it like she'd been deeply wronged, and in my heart I thought, *no more notes for me.*

But a week later, she went grocery shopping and Dad called me into my room. "Look," he said, pointing to an electrical outlet in the corner. Confused, I looked back at him, but he just smiled and walked over to it. "Don't plug anything in."

"Why?"

"Because it doesn't work anymore." He reached down and pulled the faceplate from the wall to reveal a folded piece of paper resting in the hollow, rectangular wooden box he'd built inside. "Our little secret."

We spent the next eight years leaving each other notes. Sometimes they were just pictures or a silly joke, and although I worried she'd discover the secret space, my mother never found out.

"It's still there?" Adrian asked, amused.

"Yup. Go take a peek."

"That's cool," he said, replacing the outlet cover. He returned to bed and, shortly thereafter, I fell asleep.

We met with a realtor the following day, and I admitted to her that I wasn't ready to sell the house right away.

"That's okay," she said. "It's better to wait until after the holidays anyway. Early spring would be even better."

Adrian and I went on a few errands and spent the evening ridding the house of perishable items. As I was getting ready for bed, I realized I'd run out of toothpaste and checked the guest bath for a spare tube. I thought Adrian was watching television in the basement, but I heard something coming from my bedroom. I tiptoed out to the hallway and listened. Nothing. "Adrian...?"

"Yeah," he answered, soon popping his head out from the bedroom.

"Oh, I thought you were downstairs."

"I was." He smiled.

"Okay." I stepped back into the bathroom, but something was tingling my senses. He acted the same, but when he got in the shower the next morning, I couldn't help but check the outlet.

I carefully removed the faceplate and gasped with a delight named "I knew it was you" when light from the bedside table lamp caught the sparkly contents of the faux outlet. The evidence I'd been begging the universe for had appeared, and how lovely it shined as I slipped it on my finger. At the sound of the shower turning off, I returned the ring to the box exactly the way I'd found it and busied myself with packing.

Agent Bradshaw would get a blue diamond ring along with her collar, and I'd get my life back, separate and far from Adrian. The thought should have made me ecstatic, but instead, I felt nothing, not even when I hid the ring in my bra while Adrian was loading the taxi with our luggage.

Dominic called on our way to the airport, and Adrian answered, "Thought I told you to take a few days. Two Guns can handle whatever it is."

Dom said something else, and it made Adrian's eyes widen. "Well, shit. I won't be home until dark...just handle it. I trust your judgment as always."

"How's he doing?" I asked.

"Would rather be working than sitting around."

I was quiet for a moment, but my curiosity bubbled over, and I had to ask, "Do you tell him that a lot?"

"Tell him what?"

"To just handle it."

"Yeah, I guess. I can't do everything or be everywhere, so thank God for Dom. He's my stunt double. His thoughts are my thoughts anyway."

"So he just decides things and runs them by you?"

"Sometimes. No, I don't know. We have a system. He's good to check in with me, but he has free reign. Sometimes he asks what I want him to do; sometimes I tell him. Sometimes he just figures it out himself." To hear it made me feel sick, and it took my mind to the liquor store. I wondered who'd been in charge of the system, which one of them decided that Patrick needed to feel scared. Dom said it was Adrian, but did he remember it right? Were they thinking the same thoughts that time? I wondered if it was Dominic or Adrian that hired the kid, how they even met him to begin with.

I didn't know if Adrian was guilty, but if he was, I needed him to be so entirely. The worst thought for me wasn't that he could actually be innocent, but that both of his feet were planted firmly in a murky area somewhere beyond innocence but just shy of culpability.

I boarded the plane thinking about our marriage and how it hadn't felt as strained the past few days, how Adrian was looking at me in a way he hadn't in months. *Con man. He's a con man,* I reminded myself. But still, my plan felt tattered.

Before landing, Adrian looked at me and said, "I should have been there when your dad passed."

"It's fine, really. It was a weird time."

"No, I should have been there. Not being there felt wrong."

"Wrong how?"

"I don't know. Wrong. You know when something just feels wrong?"

I did. I really, really did.

Once home, we made love, except this time I wasn't angry. I wasn't pretending he was someone else, and I wasn't lying.

PART FOUR

THIRTY-SIX

Julia

GRANT PARK IS home to some of Chicago's most notorious landmarks, and Adrian hated it. "It's too touristy. I want to be with the real Chicagoans," he'd say. Perhaps it was his distaste for the area that inclined me to choose it as a secret meeting place.

"Could you have picked a more ridiculous spot? This better be good, Julia." Dom said, loading spicy mustard onto a street hot dog.

"Let's walk."

"Fine by me." We walked until the crowd began to thin. "So is this the part where you tell me you're turning into Savannah again?"

"Not quite."

"Good, because your plans have a way of coming unstitched and catching fire."

"I know," I half-laughed. "And it's got me thinking..."

"Uh oh. About what?"

"About Savannah. I mean, who is she? She could turn out to be pretty despicable. What if I don't like her?"

"I'd say that should be the least of your concerns." He rolled his eyes and finished the last of his hot dog.

"Right. But Dom...I don't think I can do it."

"Do what?"

"All of it. Run. Start a new life. I've already done that once."

"And look how well it's turned out for you."

"I think I want to stay."

"Stay? Like in Chicago...?"

"I mean...," and it was one of the hardest things to say, "married to Adrian."

He stopped walking and wouldn't even look at me.

"Dom...Dom, say something. I know it sounds crazy..."

"No Julia, it's not crazy; it's stupid. I don't understand you. What are you thinking?"

"What were you thinking even blowing this up in the first place?"

"That you'd want to know the truth. That you *deserved* to know."

"Truth? Suddenly, for this one occasion, you became an advocate for truth? Don't act like some kind of martyr, Dom."

"Then don't act like this weak, emotionally unstable woman just wasting her life away for someone that doesn't deserve her."

"Since when are you the authority on what everyone deserves?"

"This has gone off track."

"Tell me this, Dom...and I want a straight answer."

"Sure. Whatever you want. I'll always give you whatever you want, won't I?"

"Did Adrian tell you to hire that kid, or did you think of it on your own?"

"Honestly Julia, I don't remember."

"Bull."

"It's the truth."

"It can't be. Tell me how it happened. Tell me if he ordered the hit."

"It wasn't a hit. Like I said, it was an accident. It was only supposed to be a flesh wound at most."

"But whose idea was it, yours or Adrian's?"

"I don't know."

"I'm not leaving until you tell me."

"Well then, enjoy your afternoon, because I gotta go. Adrian's waiting."

Adrian

The morning started off a nut crusher and continued going downhill from there. Meetings with the underboss usually went well for me, but the consequences of the jewelry heist had him spewing strong words from the *boss* boss. I'd given them their cut of the profits, but they were starting to feel the heat from the Feds, and of course there wasn't a thing they liked about it. On top of that, Mickey's mouth had inspired a meeting between underbosses. Mine wanted to kill him; his wanted me thrown off the plank and fed to the gators. I'd have killed Mickey a long time ago, but of course, even though he wasn't a made man, his hit wasn't sanctioned or even completely excusable.

Long story short, the boss sent down word that if I got pinched over the jewels, I was on my own. I could still use the lawyer, but I'd have to foot the bill for anything beyond the amount I'd given them for their cut of the robbery. My crew and I had been slapped on the wrist in advance, and it made my blood boil. No balls, there were absolutely no balls on these "bosses," not to mention loyalty. Blood oath my big toe. Maybe they thought it made them look tough, but I wasn't intimidated.

Intimidation is a powerful psychological tool, one I'd used to my benefit in vast and varied ways. The thing about inflicting intimidation is not that you need to know *how;* it's that you have to know *how often.* Use intimidation willy-nilly and you'll find yourself losing respect. You'll be seen as nothing but a hard-ass or, worse yet, a man trying to overcompensate. *What could he possibly be trying to make up for,* your crew will ask themselves. Suddenly, you've got a weakness, real or imagined, and that ain't good.

I'm not trying to say that a wise boss saves intimidation for a rainy day; I'm saying he doles it out conservatively. There's a difference. Use it only when the situation calls for it and you establish a certain position among your crew, your new business partners, or heck, even with a female interest.

Mickey Santino was one of my all-time favorite people to intimidate. There was something about him I liked; I think it was his love for the game. He so badly wanted to be a good gangster, but he didn't quite know how, and that last part is what made me detest him. He wouldn't get off my back about his cut of the robbery, and he did it in such an exasperating way I'm surprised I didn't kill him the second he barged into Fancy's demanding his money.

"Come on, Adrian!" He was belligerent and, from what I could tell, tweaked. "I deserve that money...you owe me big time."

"You owe me for keeping your sorry ass out of prison," I said, jaw clenched as I led him by the shirt collar through the hallway and past my office. I threw him back out into the daylight and paced around trying to calm myself down. "Come on, we're going for a drive."

"A drive?"

I shot him a heated glance until he realized we couldn't talk inside in case someone with a badge was listening. I was so paranoid by this point that I didn't even want to drive my own car, so I led Mickey across the street and said, "This one."

"What about it?"

"We're driving this one. Get it started."

"It's not my car."

"We're borrowing it, you moron."

"I don't...I don't know how to—"

"Good God," I huffed, stepping in front of him. In less than two minutes, we were on the road and I made Mickey drive.

"Geez, Adrian, where'd you learn to do that?"

The real question is, how have you made it this long without learning how to do that? "Listen, Mickey. It's like I've told you a hundred times. Except for the percentage that goes up, *no one* has gotten paid, because it's the smart thing to do."

"I've got bills, Adrian. I need that money, and you never could have pulled this off without me and Holly."

"First of all, be more like Holly. Holly's being smart about this. She understands. And second of all, you almost screwed the entire deal with that running out of gas shit! Who forgets to fill the tank before a million-dollar score?"

"Million-dollar score!" he scoffed. "That's another thing! You told me one million, but the news keeps saying four. You lied! You owe me quadruple!"

"Or what? You'll take it to the cops? Tell 'em everything? Get your own cousin locked up? That's not a way to get your money! And besides…you and Dale are the only ones who can be linked to this because of your own stupidity! The police saw your faces that night, Mickey! They know who you are!"

"Yeah well, I've seen some things of my own lately."

"Nothing I care about, I'm sure."

"Hmmm, see that's where you're wrong." He grinned, trying to act like he was holding a secret wild card, and he pulled the car into a side lot.

"When it comes to you, Mickey, I'm never wrong. Except for once, when I told Dominic that you could pull this off without a problem. I knew you were a little behind the curve, but you went and took it to a whole new level. I vouched for you, and now you're here begging for money that's not yours. You'll get what you're owed, in due time, just like everybody else."

"I need it now."

"Why is it so difficult for you to understand that I can't trust you to not go out and blow fifty-thousand dollars on something that will cause the Feds to crawl even further up my anal cavity than they already are? Dammit Mickey, did you fall out of the intelligence tree and hit every single dumb-fuck branch on the way down?"

"Funny. You're such a funny guy. Kudos to you, Adrian. But let me ask you something. If I'm so dumb and you're so smart, how come I know your best friend is in bed with your girl and you're just now finding out?"

"You're on drugs. Get ahold of yourself."

"Yeah, you know what, I'm probably full of shit. But what's

Julia up to today anyway?"

"Mention my wife one more time, I dare you."

"Now, now...," he teased, leaning toward me. "I don't mean to disrespect, but you might want to double-check her calendar. Was she supposed to be at Grant Park this afternoon? Better yet, is she supposed to be with Dominic? Because I just saw them, and by the looks of it, they were having themselves a little lovers' quarrel."

"Lovers' quarrel," I mimicked, pressing my gun into his forehead.

"Whoa. Whoa, whoa, whoa! If this is about the money..."

"It's not," I promised and pulled the trigger.

Dominic

As soon as I walked into Fancy's, Adrian stood from his chair and said, "Come on, we're getting lunch."

"I just ate."

"Then eat again," he said, clearly in a mood.

"Okay...your car or mine?"

"Yours."

We got in the car and drove to Lydia's, but other than when he called to place an order, he didn't say a word. He became more chatty after picking up the food, started asking me questions about my day.

"How'd your morning go?"

"Fine. And yours?"

"Just dandy," he deadpanned, only adding to the tension. "What did you do?"

"Went to collect a debt."

"How much did you get?"

"Nothing. Person needs more time."

"Interesting..."

"Not really."

"You said you had lunch already. What'd you have?"

"Hot dog."

"With who?"

"Myself. Did I say I wanted to play Twenty Questions?"

He didn't respond and, a moment later, I pulled the car into Fancy's back parking lot. Before I could turn off the engine, Adrian reached over, grabbed the base of my neck, and slammed my face into the steering wheel. *Boom! Boom! Boom!*

My left eye immediately began to swell; blood poured from my nose; and at least one of my teeth had broken the barrier of my bottom lip.

"I don't know what the fuck you think you're doing, but you're not doing it anymore," he said, got out of the car, and threw one of the styrofoam boxes at me through the window.

I cleaned myself and drove around the block, and although it wasn't a smart thing to do, I made a call to Julia on her regular phone, because I thought Adrian would be less likely to log it from work since he had access to the information about all of our work phones, including the one he gave Julia. She answered the phone on the third ring. "Hey Dom, I'm really sorry about earlier."

"Forget about it...not important anymore."

"Yeah it is, and I'm sorry."

"He knows."

Silence.

"Julia...?"

"He knows what?" she asked in a panic.

"He knows we met today and I don't know what else. I think you should leave...I really think you need to get out of here."

THIRTY-SEVEN

Agent Bradshaw

JULIA...JULIA...JULIA, I thought as I listened to the tap we had going on her phone. Technology had become a beautiful thing; the prospect of her leaving town was not. She'd told me about Adrian killing their neighbor's pests, but I sent her away to concentrate on the jewelry. She wanted him prosecuted for double homicide, but at the time we didn't have bodies or even names, and I could tell she was getting more and more impatient. And then her mother died, which worried me even more. Julia seemed committed to bringing Adrian down, but she was under a lot of pressure and had experienced too many emotional life changes for my comfort.

We went to the district attorney, who then put a rush on

Adrian's indictment. The best he could do was set up a hearing before the judge in forty-eight hours. I didn't think Julia had two days left in her, nor was I sure Adrian wouldn't bring her harm, so our only shot was to apprehend them both. We could hold Adrian behind bars, but for Julia, we decided on a more gentle approach. After all, we needed her to testify.

We bombarded Adrian immediately and arrested him at Fancy's just as he was getting in his car to leave. "What'd I supposedly do this time?" He wasn't a bit nervous, and it made me want to punch him.

"Do you mean other than counterfeiting, racketeering, blackmail, bribery, operating illegal online gambling, and theft?"

"No, I just mean why are you here?"

"Murder."

"According to what?" he asked as I eased him into the rear seat.

Before closing the door, I smiled, "I think you mean whom."

An hour later, I visited him in an interrogation room. "You know, Adrian, you could just confess. It might help your sentencing."

"My sentencing," he laughed. "I'm not even sure who you want me to confess to killing."

"That's what happens when you've got such a long list."

"So who did I kill?"

"Zachary DeLong and Antonio Delgado."

"Never heard of 'em."

"That usually doesn't get you very far in court."

"Then who are they?"

"The two men you shot dead in your upstairs neighbor's apartment."

"Again, never heard of 'em, and I don't know what you're

talking about."

"Oh really? Because it seems Julia is quite familiar with their final hour...so much so that she's willing to testify."

"You're bluffing," he smiled.

It brought me great joy to pull a recorder from my pocket, set it on the table, and push play. Even better was the subtle look on Adrian's face when he heard Julia's voice on the tape.

"I'm in."

"Be more specific."

"I'll help you take him down."

"Is he putting you up to this?"

"Listen, I'll get you what you need if your offer is still good."

"What can you get me now that you weren't willing to get two months ago?"

"You and I both know he's in the middle of something big."

"So again, what are you bringing to the table, Julia?"

"I know he was involved in that jewelry heist...I'll find the proof."

"And just in case you're asking yourself the same question I was..." I pressed fast forward and gave Adrian a playful wink he did not return.

"I'm curious, Julia. Why are you doing this?"

Stretch of silence.

"I'm married to the man that killed my first husband."

"And you know this for a fact?"

"For a fact. He may not have pulled the trigger, but his fingerprints are on the bullet."

"And this one is really just because I don't like you."

"Do you love him?"
"I did."

He unclenched his jaw and looked up from the table. "Can I call my lawyer now?"

"I'd like to say no, but there's this thing called the Constitution."

"Always getting in your way, I bet."

"You have no idea."

Julia

Bradshaw's crew came and took me into protective custody. "The judge approved a hearing," one of them said. "Now's your chance to testify."

"I'm not ready."

"Of course you're ready," Agent Bradshaw said when she got back to the office.

"I don't want to do this anymore."

"It would seem you don't have much of a choice."

"I can't do it."

"Perhaps knowing I just played Adrian a recording of you saying you'd help me take him down will entice you."

"Why would you do that?" I glared, stomach dropping.

"Julia, this is what you've been waiting for."

"What did he say?" I asked, imagining my limbs tied to concrete blocks at the bottom of the Atlantic.

"Not a whole lot, Julia. He's got bigger problems than you at the moment."

"I can't face him."

"Do it once and you'll never have to do it again."

"Are you sure you can put him away?"

"You saw him wrapping the bodies. It's a slam dunk."

"Where was this attitude weeks ago?"

"I'll be honest with you: I was greedy. I wanted to hit him with as many counts as possible, and at the time we didn't have names and bodies. But things are different now, and we're running out of time."

"Then make me a deal."

"I'm making you one, remember?"

"There's one more thing."

"You get protection for the rest of your life. What else do you need?"

"I want to bury my mother. The ground was frozen last week, but it's starting to warm up."

"We can arrange a proper burial when this is all over."

"You can't promise me that. Adrian's guys will know to look for me there, and you won't want to take the risk. So take me there now before it turns into a witness protection thing."

"There's not much time."

"I won't testify until that woman is six feet under."

"Fine," she sighed. "But we're making it quick. We've got court in two days."

"And what about Mrs. Witherby? Is she safe?"

"Two steps ahead of you."

⁂

"You don't seem very emotional," Agent Bradshaw said as they lowered my mother into the ground.

"We weren't that close."

"I pulled this off and you have the nerve to now tell me you weren't that close? At least shed one single tear to make me feel like a good person."

"Boo hoo," I deadpanned. "How was that?"

"Terrible."

"If you want to be a good person, give me five minutes at my parents' house."

"Don't think so."

"Come on. I'll never see it again. It's the only thing I really care about," I lied.

She looked at her watch and must have been impressed with how much time was left before our return flight. "Five minutes."

She escorted me, wouldn't even let me unlock the door myself, but once we were inside, she let me roam alone. I floated around pretending to reminisce, but when I got to my father's den, it turned into something real. I opened the desk drawer and decided to take his watch. After clasping it around my wrist, I wrote two separate notes on small pieces of paper and slid them into my coat pocket before sailing down the hallway.

I was careful to close my old bedroom door behind me and went straight to the secret outlet to put the two notes inside. The first one had a picture of two flowers smiling under the sun and said:

Daddy,
Knock, knock.
Who's there?
A little girl.

233

A little girl who?
A little girl who can't reach the doorbell.

I placed the second note on top. It said:

I love you.
Hope you'll wear your blue suit.
Love, J

I put the ring in last and walked out to Agent Bradshaw. "Let's go."

THIRTY-EIGHT

Julia

THERE ARE THINGS that shoot adrenaline straight into the human heart: coming face to face with a lion, base jumping, blue and red lights flashing in your rearview mirror—and the moment I saw Adrian walk into that courtroom.

Agent Bradshaw thought watching it on a monitor from the next room would help ease the initial shock, but I think it was about as productive as taking a shower before a crawl through a pigpen. I caught maybe an hour of sleep the night before, and like a stupid movie, it poured rain all morning. I wondered if it was a bad omen. Rain on your wedding day is supposed to be good luck, but for trials I wasn't sure, and the truth is that it didn't even matter because I wasn't dealing with what was supposed to be, I was dealing with the mob—and worse, Adrian.

The video quality wasn't good enough to make out whether he was wearing blue or black. It was the one thing I wanted to know, but when the bailiff escorted me into the courtroom, I took the stand without looking anywhere near Adrian. I just couldn't. I wasn't ready.

I was asked a series of simple questions that soon turned into inquiries of consequence.

"What was your schedule like the day of Tuesday, October 27, 2015?"

"I had a slow morning, went on a few errands, and came home in the late afternoon."

"The home you share with your husband, Mr. Adrian De Luca?"

"That's correct."

"Was he home when you got there?"

"Yes."

"Was he alone?"

"Yes," I lied.

"You're sure?" The district attorney gave me a sideways glance.

"I'm sure."

He took a pause and paced a full circle before turning to face me again. "Okay, Mrs. De Luca, at what point did your husband leave home that evening?"

"He didn't. He was with me all night."

To say he was at a loss for words would be an understatement, and to say Agent Bradshaw wasn't staring a hole right through me would be double perjury on my part.

"I'd like to remind you that you're under oath. Did you cook dinner that night?"

"Yes."

"What did you have?"

"I don't recall."

"Did your husband leave your home before or after dinner?"

"Neither. He was there all night."

"And you had no guests?"

"None."

"That's interesting," he said, plucking a piece of paper from the prosecutor's table. "Because we have a sworn affidavit from Mrs. Florence Witherby stating that on the night of October twenty-seventh, and I quote, 'Adrian invited me over for dinner and I did my needlepoint while Julia fixed dinner—eggplant parmesan, which was very good although a tad too salty.' When asked why she thought Mr. De Luca would invite her over, she responded, 'He knew I was having trouble with some little thieves who kept coming around asking for my prescriptions. The third time they came to the door, I told them no, that I needed my medicine, and one of them got real mad. I tried to calm him down, told him I didn't have any left until my new prescriptions came in, and they said fine, made me tell them when I was due for a refill, and promised they'd return. Well, I happened to mention it to Adrian the next day and he said not to worry, he'd take care of it.' So Mrs. De Luca, are you *sure* there were no guests at your dinner table that evening?"

"I'm positive."

"Then how do you explain the part where Mrs. Witherby describes that, after dinner, Adrian went to her apartment alone, and while the two of you watched *Jeopardy*, two loud thuds came from upstairs where her living room would be?"

"I don't know Mrs. Witherby very well, but I'd say she either has an active imagination or Alzheimer's."

"Do you recall leading federal officers to believe otherwise?"

"I don't."

"But you did it."

"Do you have it on tape?" I asked, surprised at my own level of arrogance.

He glared at me, and then he looked to the judge. "I can provide the court with logs and dates, Your Honor."

I was released from the witness stand but, before retreating down the main aisle, raised my glance toward Adrian. He was expressionless, but his suit, shirt, and tie—all black—said it all.

As for Agent Bradshaw, she didn't have much to say except, "Enjoy jail."

"Excuse me?"

"Remember that time you deposited dirty money into an offshore bank account? Twice? Yeah, that's a crime."

"But you knew I was doing it."

"Do you have it on tape?"

THIRTY-NINE

Dominic

"ARE YOU STUPID or just bored with your life?" I asked Agent Bradshaw as soon as she answered her phone.

"Excuse me?"

I was under her skin. Good. "Who in their right mind would give you a badge?"

"And who am I speaking with?"

"Oh, you probably recognize my voice from those fancy little bugs you rely upon so steadily. Ever thought of doin' your job the old-fashioned way?"

"Okay, fair enough. Pretty sure I know the reason for this call, so let's continue down that path, shall we?"

"Why would you put her in jail?"

"Wow, word travels fast. She crossed me, Dominic. It's that simple."

"No, you're forgetting the part where you didn't get your way, and now that she's of no use to you, you wanna beat your chest and save face. That's what this is about: elementary school paybacks."

"What's it matter to you? Other than the fact you're in love with her?"

"It's wrong."

"I'd do the same thing to you."

"You can't scare me with prison. Hell, you couldn't even scare Julia."

"She never saw it coming."

"Even more reason to hate you."

"If that's true, then why are you calling?"

"We have some things to discuss."

"I figured it was only a matter of time now that Adrian's back out on the streets. Tell me, what hellhole are you hiding out in?"

"I'm not hiding, and it's not your problem. Your problem is your own stupidity."

"Is that so? Gee, I'd love to hear more."

"Word's gonna get out that Julia's in jail, and every wife and girlfriend in this city will take notice. Don't you think they watch the news? You're sending Julia to the slaughter to stroke your own ego, but the only thing really dead is your chance of getting another woman to even think about testifying ever again. You want to be a big, bad mafia collar chaser? Guess what, you're done when these women find out Julia is behind bars. Which leads me to my second point. Get her the hell out."

"In exchange for what?"

"I'll testify about the robbery."

"The jewelry heist?"

"You know good and well that it is."

"Too late. We flipped Holly Gadaldi twenty minutes ago."

"How far do you think a junkie's testimony will go?"

"Don't lie to me."

"Okay, roll up her sleeves. I bet she's in the office right now."

"I'm not doing that."

"Fine. But when she starts twitching on the stand..."

There was a long pause, but finally she agreed. "I suppose a little backup won't hurt."

"And you'll get her out today?"

"Today. Right now."

"Good. And one more thing. I want to see her."

"That's not possible."

"Oh, I'm sure it is. Make it happen or I'm out."

"You're asking two favors with one threat. I'm gonna need something more from you."

"You remember who my father was, right? I've been his son much longer than I've known Adrian. I'll throw you some bones."

"Like what?"

"Bodies. Names. But I need to see her first."

"Been a pleasure doing business with you, Mr. Abbatelli. Be here in an hour."

I hung up the phone and dialed Two Guns.

"Dom, what's the deal? Don't tell me you turned snitch. Tell me this is a big misunderstanding." He sounded upset.

"I can't explain it now but you need to lie low. Take Tami and get out of town. That's what I would do."

"You ratted."

"No."

"But you're about to, huh?"

"Adrian lying low?"

"No Dom, he just got out of prison, and he's figuring out what to do with his ex-best friend and rat wife!"

"Tell him to be smart. They're gonna come for him again. Soon."

"If you're not a rat, then how do you know this?"

"I talked to Holly. She's acting weird. I think she flipped."

"Dammit, that's just what we need, a junkie rat."

"Be good, Tony. I gotta go." I hung up the phone and dropped it down a sewage drain.

Julia

I hadn't been in a prison jumpsuit for more than twenty minutes when a guard came into the holding area and called my name. I stood and followed him thinking I was on my way to a cell, but to my surprise, an FBI agent greeted me just outside the door. "Put these on and make it quick," he said, handing me the clothes I'd just changed out of.

Was Agent Bradshaw saying *gotcha!* or was I getting into a car with one of the federal employees on Adrian's payroll? The idea of both scenarios heightened my senses, but I felt a slight wave of calm once I realized the agent was taking me to FBI headquarters and, more specifically, Bradshaw's office.

"Miss me already?"

"Let's not get nostalgic," she said and escorted me down a hall I knew would eventually lead to a conference room.

"What's going on?"

"You've got a visitor." The way she smiled made me think for sure that it was Adrian, so when she opened the door, I was quite shocked to see Dominic sitting at the head of the table.

"I'll let you two have your moment," she said, letting the door close behind her.

"She's got a way with doom and gloom, doesn't she?"

"Dom, what are you doing? Whatever it is, don't. Don't get in bed with her."

"I know what I'm doing."

"Care to say what it is? Because it looks to me like you're selling your soul," I said, but then my eyes filled with tears. The way he looked at me was empty, like he hadn't a soul left to sell.

"Do you remember the night before the wedding?"

"How could I forget?"

"Think about the gift I gave you."

"And what a gift it turned out to be."

"Julia," he said, gritting his teeth. "Think about the gift I *tried* to give you. The way I remember it...it was the right gift at the wrong time."

"I'm not here to reminisce." I was annoyed, but he was unfazed.

"And so if you need to exchange that gift...now that the timing is better...I'm just reminding you that you can."

It clicked. He was offering an escape plan.

"Do you remember where I bought the gift? You still have their contact information?"

"I do," I said warmly.

"Good girl. If you need money..."

"I don't, but thanks."

He gave a nod, and then he looked down at the table as if he was ready for me to leave but not prepared to watch me go. "They're preoccupied, but they'll be looking for you."

"I know." I started toward the door, but then I paused and

turned, waiting for him to look at me again. "In another life, you and I..." *We could have been something,* and I knew he knew what I meant, because he nodded along and smiled.

"Yup, another life. Just not this one. And Julia..."

"Yeah?"

"We might get there sooner than you think."

I stood frozen, wanting to say that I understood, but instead I let it be as sobering as he intended. I knew what might happen, what Adrian might do once I walked outside, but Dominic knew it better than I ever could.

"If you could do it over again..."

"Thinking like that is a waste of time," he answered, sounding bitter.

"I know, but...what would you do differently?"

"Everything. Most likely nothing, I don't know. And you?"

"Same," I said and left the room, closed the door, and looked at him through the glass. With a wave, I prepared to leave, lipping the words *thank you.*

FORTY

Julia

THE ONLY THING more unsettling than walking into prison was the walk out of Agent Bradshaw's office. She'd done the fine favor of letting me call for a taxi, but past that, I was on my own.

I thought for sure Adrian's crew would be watching and waiting, and maybe they were, but I didn't spot anyone on the short walk to the taxicab. Still, I knew that not seeing them didn't mean they weren't there, so I behaved as if they were.

I had the driver drop me at a train station, where I bought an "I Love Chicago" sweater and a knitted cap I could tuck my hair into. Then I jumped on the train, switching rush hour lines until I was convinced I'd lost any tail that may have been. Finally, I emerged from the station and walked a few blocks, where I nearly cried when I saw my old house. It was still so welcoming to me, and I was glad I hadn't sold it, but I knew I couldn't go inside. Instead, I snuck around to the backyard and uncovered the box I'd buried months before.

I thought I could hear a voice but wasn't sure if it was my imagination or the neighbors. Before I could decide, a light came on inside the house, paralyzing me until I talked myself into remembering the living room lamp set on a timer. But still, I thought, *I'm dead, I'm dead, I'm dead.* I waited for movement, a shadow, anything, but there was nothing. Everything I'd buried was still there, untouched, so I took it and left, whispering good-bye with a long gaze from across the street.

Blocks away, I rented a seedy motel room—*just like every movie in the history of ever*—because I didn't know if I should use the credit card Dominic had made for me. I could trust him, but could I really? Did he actually know people Adrian didn't? Adrian could get to them, I knew he could, so I paid cash for the room and took a hot shower, but when I stepped out, there wasn't a single gun pointed at me. *Really?*

It should go without saying that I was terrified, but to what degree, I couldn't exactly say. I used to be afraid of what Adrian would do when he found out, but now that he knew everything, it wasn't death I was thinking of. It was the possibility that he would never love me again, that except for killing me, he'd never want another thing to do with me. All this time, I'd yearned for the day I could be free of him, spent months obsessed with the thought of escape, but now that I was hiding, on the cusp of being gone, I knew I wanted to be found. I was hiding from his crew but wanted Adrian to find me.

Still wrapped in a towel, I stepped around the corner and

realized a slight disappointment over the fact that no one was there. I turned on the television to drown out my thoughts: *Isn't he upset? Doesn't he want me dead? Where's his jealous rage? Didn't I mean something to him?*

I dried my hair, thinking of how Adrian always said women change their minds too often and for no logical reason, and for the first time, I agreed with him on that notion but wondered when I'd started being such a letdown to women across the nation.

I got into bed, ears burning, hoping it was Adrian thinking about me, and managed to string together a few short bursts of rest. The next morning, I called Lydia's and asked for Goldie.

"I'd like to place an order for delivery."

"Go ahead."

"I'll need a chocolate shake, no whip, three cherries." I smiled. "And I'm gonna need you to deliver it."

"Ju-," she stopped. "Oh honey, are you sure?"

"It's safe. I need you."

"Okay, baby girl. After my shift."

FORTY-ONE

Adrian

BETRAYAL NEVER COMES from your enemies. That's why the blow takes your breath away. The power of betrayal is that someone close to you has pulled the plug on what you thought could breathe on its own, and now, something you thought would go on forever has been lost.

My most significant loss came when my entire family was killed in one night, but even that wasn't betrayal. One thing about your enemies, they can never betray you. The murderers were everything I thought they were. So maybe that's betrayal's hangover: the ever-pressing realization that you made bad choices and the people you thought were one thing weren't that thing at all. You can always get revenge, but those people can never go back to what they once appeared to be—to themselves and, most painfully, to you.

It's the people closest to you that inflict the most damage, because it's the pain you least expect. The woman I loved turned against me with the help of my best friend, and nothing had ever surprised me more. There could have been no greater strike to a man like me, and it changed the way I looked at everyone, even myself.

I'd always lived by the modus operandi *shoot first; ask questions later.* But now I was paralyzed, in a way. I couldn't shoot; I was too busy asking questions, and that's how I knew it was the beginning of the end. My identity was about to change, and it had very little to do with a fake passport. I spent my whole life as a gangster or waiting to be one, so how would I become something else? How would I decide on a strategy? Was I acting as my old self, or was I already a man on the verge of nothingness?

I had to leave; I just didn't know where I'd go or what I'd do. I craved justice for myself, even if justice meant pain and suffering for the two people I loved most. Love makes hard men go soft. Betrayal turns it on its end.

Julia was the woman I'd kill for, which isn't saying a whole lot for a man like me, but the point is that I'd never imagined having to kill her. I was imagining it now, and my anger allowed me to do so in varied, imaginative ways. But still, I wondered if it would be better to kill her now or make her wait. Wouldn't it be better for her to spend the rest of her life in fear?

I had to get away from Chicago, because I knew the Feds would come for me again, and this time I wouldn't get off so easily. So I settled on leaving, knowing I'd come back, knowing I'd find her and make her life a living hell. I'd let her be for a good long while, but then I'd drop something in her path to let her know I'd been there. I'd go away and come back, go away and come back until the moment was perfect.

There was only one woman who'd always done me right, and I went to see her before leaving town. She found me waiting in her car at the end of a shift, and to my surprise she was only slightly startled.

"Hi Goldie." I smiled, looking at the reflection of those familiar eyes in the rearview mirror.

"Are you going to join me?" she asked, motioning toward the passenger seat.

"Why don't you drive a minute?"

She did as I requested, and for a few blocks, we said nothing. I eventually got out of the car and switched to the front seat. "So this is it, huh?" Her smile was sad.

"This is it. I'll be back...but it'll be a long time."

"Where will you go?"

"It doesn't matter."

"It matters to me."

"It shouldn't," I said, and I think it hurt her feelings.

"Adrian..."

"You've been good to me. I just wanted to tell you that. That's all this is."

"I'm glad. But there's something I have to tell you...it's just that I want you to promise to be good." I gave her a look that let her know I'd never made that kind of promise, and she went on to explain, with hesitation, that she'd spoken to Julia, who knew I wouldn't leave without saying good-bye to Goldie, and it got under my skin that she knew me so well.

Goldie told me where she was staying and that she wanted to see me.

"She can rot in hell, and you can tell her I said that."

"So you're not going to hurt her?"

"Not yet."

"Adrian..."

I left Goldie with a kiss on the cheek, and she told me to be careful, but careful wasn't on my mind.

The next task at hand was delivered to me by a faithful informant I'd chewed out for not knowing about Julia's cooperation with the Feds. Agent Sudeikis swore he had no idea, that even though he worked in Bradshaw's office, Julia's long-planned testimony had been kept secret from him, which was a major letdown he made up for by letting me know the time and place Dominic would be transferred from one safe house to another.

My dad never had to worry about snitches. The old-school mob was different. Back then, you didn't even *think* about flipping. You may have cheated your wedding vows or told the doctor you'd stop drinking, but you never, ever turned on the family. The finger prick healed quickly, but the blood oath was a part of you forever, and modern times had me thinking I was born in the wrong decade. But Dominic, so it seemed, belonged right where he was.

Sudeikis found out who'd be driving Dominic's Marshall car and, for a stack of Gs, convinced him to play along. He promised to pull over at an abandoned gas station and take a leak in the woods out back. I'd jump him; we'd have an altercation real enough to provide him an alibi; and then he'd pretend to be passed out while I went for Dominic.

I couldn't wait to see the look on his face.

FORTY-TWO

Adrian

DOMINIC REMAINED CALM when the agent went down. Maybe he was expecting me, or maybe he just didn't care anymore. Perhaps he'd heard that Two Guns took care of Holly. Regardless, he stepped out of the car and, in a calm way, let me take the first shot, but after that it became a two-sided exchange.

Fighting each other felt awkward and right at the same time, but both of us were eventually bleeding and out of breath, so we stood to our feet and faced each other. "If your father was here to see this...he'd either stroke out again or wish he was dead," I said.

"Well if anyone would know, it'd be you Adrian. He always

was more your father than mine, wasn't he?"

"Is that what this is all about? Poor little Dom and his daddy complex?"

"That was a long time ago."

"Yeah and you said you were good. Remember? Remember when I said, 'Hey Dom, I know this is a little awkward,' and you said, 'Don't worry about it, I'm fine,' and then acted like you never wanted to be made in the first place?"

"I *was* fine! What else was I supposed to be? What other choice did I have?"

"To tell me, to tell the truth for one second!"

"Oh, I've been livin' my truth. But what about you, Adrian? What about your daddy? The saint you run yourself ragged trying to live up to. What would he think about you abandoning his city and running this one into the ground?"

"Oh, it's me, huh? I ruined Chicago? And you would have done it better, is that what you mean?"

"I mean we're never coming back from this, Adrian. Not this family. Not this round. We're done. I can't follow these people. These aren't our fathers and grandfathers. These aren't gangsters. And you know what, neither are we...not anymore."

"Don't say we. Don't bring me into this."

"It's not what it used to be and you know it."

He was right, but I wouldn't admit it. For a while, we were gangsters, back when it meant something, but now we were broken sons. "You break my heart."

"Yeah well, leaving it unsaid won't undo it."

"That's not what I meant."

"Then just kill me. That's what you came here for."

"No...I came to see you one last time before you live the rest of your life a coward."

Not once had I come so close to killing someone without actually doing it, but I didn't want to live with Dominic's blood on my hands.

As I was leaving him that day, he said, "I loved you, Adrian. Still do." It stopped me in my tracks, but I stood with my back to him, never turning to look at him when I decided to keep walking, because I physically could not utter the words *I loved you too*. Or was it love?

Hours later, I sat on a grounded private jet, considering what had transpired. I make decisions quickly and change them slowly, but this time the regret came almost immediately. *I should have killed him. I let him off too easily.* I'd made the right choice, but it felt wrong, so much so that it made me step off the plane. I couldn't make the same mistake with Julia.

FORTY-THREE

Julia

GOLDIE TOLD ME what Adrian said, but I didn't know what it meant. I didn't know if he was telling her what she wanted to hear or if he truly did plan to leave me alone. Devoid of appetite but full of nervous energy, I waited, but he never showed. I really thought he would come for me, and the fact that he didn't was somehow worse than any of the terrible punishments he might have given.

Dominic was testifying and it would happen soon, so I knew Adrian would hit the road. He was likely on his way out of town, if not already gone, and his guys would either be playing it safe or too busy helping him to care about me, so I called it.

After organizing what few belongings I had, I walked to the

front office to settle my tab. Distracted by the idea of plan B, I bought three bottles of water from the vending machine and miserably returned to my room, its crooked, rusty 7 hanging on the door by only one screw. I'd left it unlocked for myself and stepped inside only to jump out of my skin.

There, sitting in the corner chair, was Adrian staring fire right through me. He was brooding but still, which petrified me to no end, and yet there was joy in it. This was it. I was either dead or slowly coming back into his good graces, but it was impossible to decipher which.

"Why'd you throw your testimony?" he asked without a flinch. "I wore the black suit."

"So you did get the note."

"Was it out of fear? Were you scared?"

"I was tired."

"Of what?"

"Being...so far away from you." For half a second he started to smile, but then it seemed he remembered that he should be angry.

He pointed to my bag and asked, "Going somewhere?"

"Adrian, I was wrong." It was one of the only statements I could recall from the thousands of lines I'd practiced.

"About that hat you're wearing?"

"No." I sort of laughed and then grew serious. "About... thinking you killed Patrick."

"Oh, I killed Patrick." He stared with intent, studying my reaction. "Not with my own hands, but..."

"I know. You're not the man I made you out to be."

"I'm a little bit of that man, Julia." He said it with a slight wince, studying me again.

"I know. I knew it before."

"Good. Because I'm not here to apologize..."

"Then why are you here?"

"You invited me, didn't you?"

"Why'd you show up?"

"Because I was on a plane trying to leave...but I couldn't."

"Why not?"

"Where would I go without you?" He said it bluntly, forcing tears of relief down my cheeks.

"Do you think you'll ever forgive me?" I asked.

"I could ask you the same question." He smiled. Then he stood and slowly made his way to me. With a tug on my chin, he pulled my lips to his.

"What now?" I asked, still trembling.

"Did you pack running shoes?"

"Did you pack swim trunks?"

"I *knew* you'd say tropics."

"I think I have a ride. Dom set me up with a guy..."

"You've learned nothing, both of you. I've taught you nothing."

"What? It's a way out."

"I'm not using Dom's guy. Besides, I've got my own."

"Bet you a thousand bucks it's the same guy."

"It's not. I guarantee it."

"Fine." I smirked.

"We're wheels up ASAP, okay? We can't stop at the house."

"Deal. Where are we going?"

"Where do you want to go?"

"The islands."

"The Feds have the money by now."

"Yeah, I'm sure they do. Part of it at least." I grinned.

"What do you mean? Where's the other part?"

"You've learned nothing. I've taught you nothing," I teased.
"You didn't put it all in the account..."
"Nope."
"So in other words, I taught you something after all."
"Not what I said. I'm bringing cash. What are you bringing?"
"Cash. And this," he said, holding the blue diamond ring.
"Didn't think I'd see that again." I smiled.
"That makes two of us."

We summoned Goldie and sold our homes to her for one dollar each, which left her in rare form. She was stunned and flailing around like only she could do, but when she finally turned to go, she knew we were leaving and that we'd never be back. It was the only good-bye I truly regretted. I wish we'd have taken her with us, and I thought about her almost every day.

As for my parents' house, I did nothing. I could practically hear my mother turning in her grave. Deserting that house was a sad thought, but in due time, when I'd been gone long enough, it would be auctioned or something of the sort, and Mrs. Shirley would help. I reminded myself that my father wasn't there. It wasn't his house; it had always been Helen's. Daddy's house was the bank and the ballpark—memories that wouldn't fit in a suitcase, but I could take them with me.

We got a ride, hours out of the city, to a barely there runway sitting on the back lot of a mansion, not wasting any time on our walk to the plane awaiting our arrival. *It's not what you know,* Adrian had always said. *It's who.*

"Wheels up?" the pilot asked.

Just then, Adrian's phone rang. He showed his index finger

and answered, "What's good?"

I nudged him, and for once he put the call on speaker. It was Two Guns. "He gave the testimony."

"So it's done?"

"It's done. But Adrian, he didn't give you up."

"What do you mean? He gave the testimony. They're coming after me."

"Yeah, but when they asked if it was you who attacked the Marshall vehicle, he said it wasn't."

"Yeah?"

"Yeah. Said it couldn't have been you 'cause, in his words, the person who hit him hit hard and you've always hit like a little pussy."

Adrian chuckled, his eyes a flash of entertained sadness. "Take care, Two Guns."

"Take care, my man. Hey wait...what about Julia? We didn't find her."

"I did. I took care of it."

"Oh. Okay boss..."

"Stay away from those horses...they'll be looking for you at the tracks." In a daze, Adrian shut the phone, took my hand, and said, "Wheels up."

FORTY-FOUR

Julia

WE FLEW TO a distant island of the Cooks, maybe because we figured no one would think us dumb enough to go there, maybe because it just felt right. When the plane touched down, I looked at Adrian and said, "One more question."

"You better do it before we get off this plane."

"Did you know it was him?" I asked, meaning Patrick.

"No."

"Not even an inkling? Ever?"

"I missed it, Julia. There was too much going on."

I nodded and thought the conversation was over, but then he said, "Now one for me."

"Okay."

"Did you love him?" This time he meant Dom.

"Not like that. Not like you. And nothing ever happened between us."

We had enough money to live simply but comfortably and bought a charmer of a house a short walk from the water, deciding to introduce ourselves as Bill and Anita Golden, "ex-rat racers," pun intended for our own personal humor.

Of all the unthinkable, improbable things I'd seen, watching Adrian defect topped the list. Running had never been his forte, so I used terms like "starting over" or "living the island life," because they sounded exciting and luxurious, less cowardly. But in the beginning, whether brought on by guilt or second-guessing or just plain shock, there was something dead inside him and I knew it was because of Dominic. We thought about but never spoke of him, and both seemed right.

Adrian mentioned his parents only occasionally but more often than before. I asked what they would think about our life now, but he didn't know. He was torn. Weeks later, at the end of a perfect day, we built a fire on the beach and stayed there until the final ember was no more. "You know what I think they'd say?" he asked.

"What's that?"

"They'd say 'good for you.'" He smiled, grabbed my hand, and walked me home.

I think he was right, but there was more to it. His dad would have asked about business, and Adrian would fill him in on new endeavors. You could change Adrian's locale, trade in his suit jacket for a Tommy Bahama button-up, but he'd still be packing heat underneath, and his eyes and ears would always be open. We didn't necessarily need the money, but Adrian still loved to make a buck, and he did. No matter what it was—coconuts, sunscreen that supposedly repelled sand, seashell necklaces—he peddled it all and paid our neighbor, Julius, to do so.

"You think he's making the correct change?" I asked, thinking of his slight mental handicap.

"He can make change just fine, babe."

"How do you know he's bringing you all the money?"

"There's honesty in his eyes. Besides...I'd kill him if he shortchanged me."

I rolled my eyes.

"Come on, I'm kidding..." He winked, but I wasn't so sure.

Julius went to the tourist areas almost every day, and everything was going well until the time he came back earlier than usual, looking rattled. Apparently he'd been selling goods up and down the beach, like always, when someone bumped into him and sent the merchandise toppling into high tide. Much of it was lost, but poor Julius was able to save a small portion. As we laid the puka shell necklaces out to dry, Adrian assured him he wasn't upset and that everything would be fine. "Accidents happen."

"No accident, boss. He done it on purpose."

"Who? Who did it on purpose?"

"That Murphy man's son, Bradley."

Adrian was livid. "You did the right thing, Julius. I'm glad you told me. Don't worry, I don't think this will happen again. I'm *sure* it was an accident." But we both knew it wasn't. The "Murphy man" was Adrian's direct competition and likely disenchanted over the upheaval of his precious souvenir monopoly.

"Let it go," I whispered to Adrian through gritted teeth, but even though he nodded along, I knew he wouldn't listen. It's just that I hadn't expected to find proof of it at church the following Sunday.

We arrived at the service just in time, and right off the bat,

Pastor Alvez took the podium to deliver solemn news: "As many of you may have already heard, Brother Murphy and his son Bradley have been missing since Friday."

I shot Adrian a look—*what is wrong with you?*—but he ignored me.

"As they often do, they took their fishing boat out for the afternoon, and they haven't been heard from since. I paid a visit to Mrs. Murphy, and she is of course very upset and hoping for a miracle. At this time, I'd like to ask our newest deacon, Brother Bill, to lead us in prayer."

Adrian nodded as if there was nothing he'd rather do more. Then he stood and cleared his throat. "Dear Lord, we come before You today with great concern for two of our own. May You bring us comfort and great faith. Like Mrs. Murphy, we want a miracle, but most of all, we want *Your* will. It's in *Your* hands now. We don't know what has happened to them, but if they are still alive, let them be reminded of how much they love to fish. Perhaps they stumbled upon a great catch for which they simply were no match. We hope to find them safe, but if such things are not to be, we pray they are with You now, Lord...dining on the best of the sea, telling stories about the fishing trip of a lifetime. In Your *just* name we pray, amen."

I spent the rest of the service fidgeting, and as we left, an elderly church member walked up to us and said, "Beautiful prayer, Brother Bill, just beautiful."

"He certainly does have a way with words," I said through a jaw-clenching smile.

"True indeed. What do you think has happened to them?"

"Hard to say for sure." Adrian shrugged. "All I know is that the Lord works in mysterious ways."

"Oh yes, yes He does," she said and allowed Adrian to walk

her to her bicycle.

Fishermen spotted the Murphys the next morning and brought them to shore. As it turned out, they experienced engine failure sometime into their trip and spent three days drifting and floating but, thankfully, survived. Adrian went with Pastor Alvez to visit them in the hospital. I don't know where he got the nerve or what he said to those malnourished bullies who'd found themselves bullied, but wouldn't you know it, no one bothered Julius again.

Other than these sporadic incidences, Adrian and I live a simple life much different than anything either of us has ever known. We've settled in, and yes, we have eyes in the back of our heads, which remain on a constant swivel, but our days are peaceful and happy.

I really think we could stay here forever, but I sometimes worry that Adrian will get bored. I have nightmares that he leaves and finds a place to be a gangster again or that someone finds us out. I think of Patrick and wonder what we'd be had he never glanced into that alley or had Benny never stolen the money. I've forgiven Adrian, but on my worst days, I resent him. I resent that Patrick and Julia Hamilton are gone. There are days I even resent that Adrian and Julia De Luca are no more. Even though we left a life I was happy to abandon, I hate that we had to run, that our options are now so limited. All in all, I resent this existence of looking over my shoulder. But that's the worst of it, and I remind myself that what we did, this life we now lead, was once only a faraway daydream.

These days we're pretty good at being Bill and Anita Golden, and our regrets are nothing but fleeting moments, because we know it all turned good. We had a baby girl and named her Lydia. I try every day to be myself, and Adrian seems happy to give Lydia the life he never could have before. He didn't take it well when she started kindergarten; he couldn't sleep the entire first week. Neither of us wanted her out of our sight, so I started volunteering at the school as often as possible, but it was only slight relief.

By Christmas of that first school year, the man who served as both janitor and groundskeeper retired. Guess who took his place. Lydia, at five years young, did the thing no one else could, and turned her father into an honest workingman. Seeing Adrian in a nine-to-five is pure entertainment for me. He watches that place like a hawk, and the school's lawn has never been so meticulously groomed.

Some people call me Annie, and I answer to it with a smile. The woman they know is very much like Julia Hamilton, and I sometimes wonder what they would do if they knew the truth. I wonder if I'll ever talk about it again, if Lydia will ever know what her parents once were. I think about the future and what my daughter's safety has to do with our past, wondering if she would benefit from knowing the story in its entirety. Sometimes I practice that story in my head, struggling over where to begin and what to leave out, if anything, which always leads me to *the devil you know is better than the devil you don't.*

Perhaps I'll tell her—on my death bed, I'm hoping—that things haven't always been this way, that life hasn't always been this clear, and that there was a time when the devil I knew...was me.

ACKNOWLEDGEMENTS

A huge thanks and appreciation goes to my readers, family, and friends for showing interest in my work and for planning to read whatever comes next before even knowing what it's about. That in itself is a hope realized and brings an extra element of enjoyment to the writing.

Thank you, as always, to my first line of readers, Jennifer, Kari, and Mom, and to my editor, Audra, for being the best, most speedy dream come true.

Thank you from the bottom of my heart to all the places I've ever called home. Your unwavering support and enthusiasm are this writer's lifeblood.

I continue to be grateful to God and country for the ability and freedom to choose this path. I'm inspired to keep getting better, to keep stretching the limit on what I think myself capable of, and to venture into projects that were once a mere daydream.

Thank you for reading my stories and sharing yours with me.

LET'S STAY CONNECTED

If you enjoyed *The Devil I Know*,
please leave an Amazon or Goodreads review
and consider sharing with your friends.

Reader photos are encouraged
and appreciated—tag them
and find Bess online here:

bessrichards.com

http://instagram.com/bessrichardsauthor

http://twitter.com/Bess_Richards

http://facebook.com/bessrichardsauthor

Receive exclusive updates
regarding new releases
by signing up for the newsletter
at bessrichards.com

ABOUT THE AUTHOR

Bess Richards lives in Pensacola, Florida with her husband.

NEVER THE SAME

The differences between all-American midwest farm kid, Briggs Sullivan, and silver-spooned city slicker, Lucy Cartwright, are undeniable, but when they meet in Times Square on New Year's Eve, the attraction between them is instantaneous. As they delve into a long-distance romance, Lucy's haunted past underscored by a depressed, absent mother and a workaholic father with a huge secret, seems, for the first time, alleviated. But, just nine months after their first meeting, September 11, 2001 comes along, derailing in every way Briggs and Lucy's plan for happily ever after. Laugh, cry, and fall in love with these characters as they tell a powerful story about love and family amidst the all too real, yet unimaginable circumstances of terrorism, war, illness, and separation. By novel's end, you'll see the mess within the picture perfect, high-values Sullivan family, and the love you weren't sure existed among the dysfunctional, despondent Cartwrights.